Crushin' On A Boss 4:

The Streets or Love

The Finale

A Novel By

Tysha Jordyn

Legal Notes

ISBN: 1541163141
ISBN-13: 978-1541163140

Dedication

In loving memory Alfonso Slaughter, Sr.

You left fingerprints of grace on our lives.

You will never be forgotten.

Rest in paradise, wise king ...

Text ROYALTY to 42828
to join our mailing list!

Text GETLIT to 22828 to
join our mailing list!

To submit a manuscript for our review, email us
at submissions@royaltypublishinghouse.com

PREVIOUSLY IN PART 3

Aniqa

"No more juice, TJ. If you're thirsty, take this."

Beautiful held up a small bottle of water for TJ. Like he'd done a half an hour earlier, he turned his little nose up and started pouting, squeezing his eyes together like he was willing a few tears to fall and hopefully snag his mom's sympathy.

"Tyleek Assad, you got about five seconds to fix your face before I give you somethin' to cry about."

Hearing the bass in his mama's voice, TJ got himself together real quick and slow-walked back over toward the jungle gym, where Essence was climbing.

"I swear that boy irks me, walkin' around here lookin' like his ugly ass daddy." Bee rolled her eyes as I stifled a laugh. "What? That nigga is ugly...can't stand his ass."

"You, Bee. That's what."

Whatever, girl, I thought to myself while shaking my head at the delusion my girl refused to abandon. I don't know who she thought she was fooling, but she knew just as well as I did that Tyleek could die several horrible deaths and probably still be fine in her eyes — that's why he had her heart for so long.

"Those two are a handful together, huh?" my mom chimed in.

Promise and I had been pretty much inseparable since the night of my surprise birthday party, aside from the time she was required to report and check-in at the sober living home where she was staying. She had to stay there for a minimum of 90 days, and if the counselors felt she'd made adequate progress, they'd allow her to move on and get her own place.

"A handful and then some," Bee replied. "Matter fact, lemme go over here and keep an eye on them in case TJ is feelin' himself a little too much and calls himself having a tantrum behind some damn juice." Bee smacked her lips and stood up from the bench. I knew she was trying to give me and my mom some time to chat privately, and I appreciated her for that.

"Baby, thanks so much for letting me come with y'all today. I know I got a lot to make up for, and I 'preciate you even giving me a chance," Promise spoke.

"Thank you for wanting to come. I appreciate that, and

it's good for Essie too."

My face said all was well in my world, but that wasn't exactly how I felt sitting there across from a woman I hadn't seen in years. So much had happened in such a small stitch in time, and whenever my thoughts got too quiet, I found my mind drifting in an effort to make sense of it all. I couldn't pretend like it didn't bother me that Essence had lost both her grandmother and father in a matter of months, because it did. Lord knows they deserved what they got, but I just didn't want Essence to miss out on anything by not having them around. It felt like just the right time for Promise to come back into my life since she was really all Essence had left as far as a grandparent. I just hoped she would be around for a while. I still couldn't wrap my mind around how Linc was able to find my mother in a matter of months when I'd gone all this time fearing that she was dead, but I was grateful he cared enough to give me that piece of my family back.

"Aniqa, I know I owe you so much, and I don't want you to feel like I'm after anything, or like I have some sort of agenda..."

"I mean... I hope that's not why you're here, but I do have a question."

I had to pause and pull my thoughts together because just tasting the words that dangled on the top of my tongue stirred a cauldron of emotions, most of which left me feeling anything but open-minded and receptive to how she would reply.

"Why now? Why did you stay away all that time? Why didn't you come back for me?"

My voice was almost pleading for some sort of explanation, though there wasn't really anything she could say to undo the years of hell I'd had to endure with Je'Marcus and his family. Still, I needed to know...

"Honestly baby, I didn't want to come back until I got myself together...I didn't want you to see me like that."

Promise fell quiet as a cloud of silence seemed to ingest our verbal exchange. My eyes frantically searched hers, easily connecting with the pool of sorrow and regret that lay beyond. Allowing her words to sink in, I had to admit that it felt like a bullshit excuse. I loved Essence more than the air I breathed, and I couldn't imagine just leaving her and staying gone for so long. I felt like a part of me would always feel empty and might even die if I wasn't able to see and hold her every day. She was a part of me, came from me, and there's no way anything or anyone could ever be important enough for me to leave her. Still, I knew everyone had a different path to walk in life, and a different set of choices to make. I'd already lost so much time with my mom, and I didn't want to waste time on being mad or stuck on the fact that she left—something neither of us could change.

"I know that may sound like a bunch of bullshit to you, Aniqa, but it's the truth and if there's one thing I've learned, it's that even when everything else is gone, you still have your truth," Promise went on to explain, her eyes sending a plea of forgiveness that stirred the embers of an unconditional love in jeopardy.

Forgiveness isn't for others; it's for you. Without it, you consent to hold your happiness hostage. Ms. Khadra's words always felt like food for the soul, always giving me just the right nudge at just the right moment.

"Well, I want you to spend as much time with Essence as you can, but I have to be careful about what and who I have her around. It's not that I don't trust you around her, but I don't want her to start getting attached to you and then have you up and disappear again. I don't want that for her," I spoke what I'd been thinking since she asked to see Essence the night of my surprise birthday party.

"That's fair, baby. I understand that, and I know it might not mean much at this point, but you have my word that I'm clean and I'm not going anywhere. That little doll is too precious for me to even think about leaving." She smiled as she looked across the way, where Beautiful was helping

Essence cross the monkey bars.

Too precious for me to even think about leaving. Hearing her say that, I felt a twinge of jealousy in my gut as I wondered where that same vow of *not going anywhere* was when I needed her. I must have drifted further into my thoughts than I realized because all of a sudden, Promise was waving her hand in front of my face.

"What'd you say?" I asked.

"I asked if you were okay..."

"Oh. Yeah, I'm fine."

"Aniqa, I know I gave you more bad than good things to remember me by, but I hope you know that I never stopped loving you. Never stopped thinking of you. Sometimes... it's just easier to stay away than to fight what you feel is a losing battle, you know what I mean?" Promise continued.

I just nodded my head because I didn't want to have to verbally admit that I knew exactly what she meant. I tried to fight back the first time Je'Marcus came at me sideways, but when I woke up to both him and his mama standing over me and telling me I'd better learn my place, I quickly realized that it would be easier to just go with the flow.

"So, tell me, how are you dealing with Shirlene and Je'Marcus being gone?" my mother asked, and just the mention of their names gave me a tension headache.

"I mean, I'm not gonna lose sleep over it. It is what it is," I spoke with my gaze fixed on Essence going down the slide; she was so happy now, so full of joy, so... free.

"Yeah... I don't wish death on nobody, but those two?"

Promise got quiet and shook her head, and I had a whole new set of questions because I didn't know a whole lot about the friendship that her and Je'Marcus' mother, Shirlene, supposedly had back in the day. Hopefully, my mom would have some of those answers.

Just the notion of taking that trip back down memory lane agitated me, but I knew I'd have to deal with it at some point. I got quiet, though, because I didn't want to ruin the day. Today was supposed to be about new beginnings, about taking the first step to give Essence something I never had. Promise must have sensed that I needed a moment because she left me to my thoughts and turned her attention to Beautiful and the kids.

I used my phone as a distraction and scrolled through my notifications, finding that I had a missed text from Linc. Linc, my happy place in what used to be a stormy life. I was seeing the sun shine a lot more lately, feeling its warmth seep into the folds of my skin and make me feel... alive.

I shot Linc a response to let him know that everything was okay. He was proving more and more each day that he really loved me and Essence, and I felt so lucky to have him. Never did I imagine some guy would come along and be able to not only accept Essence, but spoil and love on her like she was his own. Linc was happy to see that Promise had completed the treatment program he got her into, but he said that he knew addicts were always one hit from a relapse, so he didn't want me to dive in headfirst and expect a perfect ending.

I also had a text from Paxton asking how me and Essie were doing, so I shot him a quick reply as well. Things still weren't the same between us as before, but I was able to breathe a little easier knowing that there was no tension between him and Linc – at least, I didn't think there was. Beautiful joked that Paxton probably still had a lil' crush on me, but if so, I guess he found a way to brush it off or push it to the back of his mind. Just the fact that Linc welcomed him at my party was a sign that he somewhat trusted Paxton, and he damn sure wouldn't have been at the party if Linc thought for a second that Paxton would try to push up on me.

Swiping to my social media notifications, I saw that I was tagged in a picture and opened the notification, only to wish that I'd kept right on scrolling and ignored it. Sitting next to some kind of makeshift shrine with a big picture of Je'Marcus surrounded by candles was Toya. She was holding a beautiful baby boy in her arms, and my jaw dropped when I zoomed in to get a better look; her baby was the spitting image of Je'Marcus, and I almost thought I was looking at a picture of Essence as an infant. Even more striking than the mini-clone of Je'Marcus was the caption Toya had posted with the picture that read:

RIP to the last of the few. So blessed that God gave me a piece of you before he called you home. We fall, but we rise...eye for an eye, flame for a flame... karma's on her way #karma #revenge #lifeforalife #shotsfired

I read between the lines real well, and this was exactly why I wanted Linc to just let things be and let the courts deal with Je'Marcus. Now, we were about to be caught up in some tit for tat shit, and that didn't sit well with me since the police still didn't seem to have any leads on who snatched my baby.

Will I ever have a moment of peace that lasts longer than just a few seconds?

Linc

"Aight, well I don't know how long I'll be, but you need me to bring anything back?"

I was waiting for Pops and Savage to show up so we could talk about what our next move was gonna be. For once, me and Savage were on the same page about how to deal with Kappo. I felt like we knew most of what the nigga had been up to, and just that part was enough to make me wanna dead his ass. Pops was always the voice of reason, though, and what he said made sense: we needed to get as much info out of the nigga as we could to make sure we didn't have any more surprises.

"Uhh, nothing really, I think we're all good— oh, wait! Can you grab some popcorn? The movie theater butter kind?"

Aniqa made a pouty face like she thought I'd say no. She'd been on cloud nine lately, and I didn't want to do anything to pull her down. I don't know if she knew it, but she could get just about anything out of me right now.

"Aight, you got it. What's short stack doin'?" I asked as I caught a glance at what looked like Essence's little head fly by.

"See for yourself," Aniqa smiled before she switched the

camera view on her phone. Sure enough, I could see Essence running back and forth and laughing like the whole room was tickling her.

"Aww, that's what's up. Looks like she havin' a ball," I laughed.

"Man, is she? All thanks to you," Niq winked. "Linc, I just... thank you so much."

"YINC!" I heard before my view changed to the ceiling, then Essence's face came into view.

"What's up, Princess?"

She started blushing right away.

"You keepin' everybody in line?"

Seeing her nod her head at my question, I shook my head like I'd been doing ever since she decided to surprise and bless us with her sweet lil' voice.

"You're a big girl, so you gotta use your words, right?"

She let out this long, dramatic sigh, like she was hearing my words for the umpteenth time — just like her mama did when she didn't wanna hear what I was saying.

"Yesssss."

"Okay, so what are y'all doin' over there?" I furrowed my

brow, still smiling.

"Pwayin'!" Essence squealed. "Bye, Yinc!" She threw her little hand up and waved before she took off running; the phone's camera returned to its original position and Niq came into view.

"I'mma grab my princess some candy since she's doin' such a good job of keepin' y'all busy," I chuckled.

"Unt uh— NO! I'm not about to be up all night with her because of a damn sugar rush!" Aniqa squinted her eyes at me.

"Aight look, I gotta go, but hit me if y'all need anything."

"We're good, and hey— be careful." Niq smiled and blew me a kiss before she ended our FaceTime call.

Aniqa shared with Beautiful that her birthday party was one night she'd never forget, and that's just how I was hoping the night would go. Every time the subject of her mom came up, she always got this sadness in her eyes that stayed there for a few days; I hated seeing it and wanted to be able to give her something every female needed: a mom. It took some digging, but Savage was able to find Promise, Niq's mom, and though she was trying to get clean on her own, she still had a long way to go.

The first time I met Promise, I saw right away where

Aniqa got those eyes from, and there was no way I could just leave her out there damn near livin' on the streets. She agreed to go into the program I'd linked her up with, and I promised her that the day she got clean, I'd be there to pick her up and make sure she got to see Aniqa — but she had to get completely clean first. I was still learning about Niq, but I knew she'd been let down too many times in her past, so I didn't want to bring this person back into her life and set her up for more disappointment. Fast forward a few months, and I was able to give my lady a present she'd never forget.

"You done cakin', nigga? Cause if so, we ready to get started," Savage teased as him and Pops walked into the conference room and joined me at the table.

"Gone with all that, bruh." I waved him off.

"This family man thing is a good look for you, Son. Real proud of you," Pops chimed in.

"No doubt," I agreed, nodding as I slid my phone back into my pocket to give Pops my full attention.

"He ain't talkin', so what's next?" Savage took the lead, referring to how Kappo had basically been giving the crew his ass to kiss.

Savage had a crew sitting on Kappo's house, and they snatched him up one night as he was coming back from the liquor store. Hearing that he wasn't talking had me even more tight because it meant the nigga didn't think we would do shit. I needed to hear the whole story on why the fuck he did some foul shit like having Essence snatched up, only to turn around and let her go; shit just didn't make sense and made me feel like he wasn't through with whatever the fuck he had planned. I still hadn't told Niq that we knew who took baby girl, and I didn't wanna say anything until I had more answers for her because she'd def wanna know why, who, how — the whole nine.

"Tell you what. Leave Kappo to me; I need your attention on three other things. One: LaMique. I'd have her come home so we can get to the bottom of all this, but it makes more sense for her to stay out that way and you make the flight out there. That way, if something's off, she'll be able to point it out quicker than either of us. Two: this Jason kid. He might be able to give us the answers Kappo won't, and I doubt he's got the balls to play the tough guy role. If so, well, you two know what to do: plan B. Three: this Tiara girl. She knows too much, has seen too much, and you need to handle that before the law has another reason to go digging through my shit," Pops instructed, and Savage and I both nodded our agreement.

I already had a plan for Tiara's ass, but I had to be careful how I went about it because until I knew exactly what her connection was to Kappo, I couldn't risk any more fuck-ups. Bitch was under my skin like a damn fungus, but she had a bit of an advantage — for the moment. I definitely couldn't mention anything to Niq about Tiara because, again, I didn't even have all the answers for her. The last thing a nigga needed was Niq and Bee tryin' to put their heads together on some *get-back* shit. We also needed to move with caution because with Tiara being Bee's cousin, we didn't need Bee gettin' caught up in no shit just because they were related.

"I need you to stick close to Marshall's boy as well, Son," Pops ordered, referring to Paxton.

Since all this shit came to light regarding Kappo, Paxton's dad had been reaching out to Pops more. The plan was to keep the deal with Megga intact, so Pops definitely needed some eyes on the back-end of things, and Patrick Marshall was Pops' solution. I still felt like we needed to dig a lil' bit more and make sure Patrick wasn't being a snake to the snake, but so far, he seemed legit and his moves matched his words.

I had eyes on Paxton too since he was basically his dad's right-hand. I wanted to see where his head was at, particularly when it came to Niq. I knew they had a lil' friendship and whatnot, so I knew Niq might've shared some personal shit with him that she didn't think would cause any harm at the time. Where Pops was concerned about making sure Patrick was straight, I was more focused on making sure the nigga Paxton wasn't tryin' to come at Niq on no foul shit.

Bitter bitches caused drama, but bitch niggas were just as bad, and I needed to make sure I could keep Niq and baby girl out of harm's way. The way I saw it, the easiest way to do that was to stick close to Paxton until I knew where his head was at for sure. I'd act like the nigga was the homie as long as I needed to in order to make sure he was a stand-up dude and had gotten over whatever the fuck he thought he was gonna have with Niq at one point in time.

I nodded at Pops to let him know I had shit under control.

"Good, then it's all set. Linc, you're taking the red eye out tonight heading to Colorado. LaMique doesn't know you're coming, but the team hasn't really had much to report, so I don't think you'll run up on anything too out of the norm," Pops explained.

Since finding out about the shit Kappo had been up to, Pops put some guys in place to watch Mique so we could see if she was involved in his shit in any way; so far, it looked like things between them didn't go any further than the bedroom.

"Uhh, can it wait until the morning, Pops? I kinda gotta

tend to some things tonight."

I'd just made a promise to Niq about tonight, and I wasn't tryin' to ruin her high with havin' to fly out for who knows how long.

"It can't, so kiss your lady and the little one goodnight and be on that flight."

Savage's phone started vibrating on the table, so Pops used that interruption to make his exit.

"I'll leave you fellas to it." Pops turned to make eye contact with me. "Son, let me know when you land," he ordered before he left the conference room.

"Shit, man. This timing ain't 'bout shit," I complained.

"Got that shit right." Savage continued to frown as he typed out a text.

"Everything straight?" I asked.

"Nah, not at all. Emani was rushed to the hospital; somebody gotta go get lil' man," Savage groaned. "And Bee was supposed to come kick it at my spot tonight," he finished.

Chapter One

Linc

Fuck!

I called myself dressing warm so I would be prepared for the cool temperatures I'd be met with in Colorado, but the gusty winds dancing across the tarmac at Denver International disrespected the shit outta my so-called winter coat.

"What! What happened?! What's wrong, Linc?" Aniqa panicked at my outburst.

"It's cold as shit! That's what, ma." I frowned.

Don't get me wrong, I was more than prepared to put in whatever work was necessary to get shit back to normal with our business, but Pops owed me a serious solid for taking this L.

"Damn, don't scare me like that, bae!" Aniqa barked in my ear.

"No no, Yinc!" I heard Essence's little voice chime into our conversation from the background. "No no!"

"The hell?" My scowl deepened as I glanced at my watch to check the time. "The hell is she doing still up?"

I'd taken the last flight out of Norfolk International, which departed just after 11 p.m., so I saw that it was well after 2 a.m. on the East coast as I stood there being finessed by the icy night air.

"Oh, you mean this toddler turn-up she calls herself having? That's what a handful of sour Skittles does to a four-year-old right before bedtime."

I didn't have to lay eyes on Niq to see the irritation on her face. I could also see the lil' eyeroll she was giving me through the phone; it was the same one she always threw my way when she called herself checking me for spoiling baby girl.

"Shit, in that case, turn up, short stack." I chuckled as I rubbed my hands together, trying to spark up some extra body heat. I hoped my ride was waiting out front like Pops said because a nigga was about to freeze!

"Uh huh, well I'm gonna make sure you get a big ass side of this toddler turn-up when you get back."

"Nah, I'm good on that, but speakin' of big ass—"

"Bye Linc, I'm not about to play with you. Call me when you get checked in, okay? We love you," Niq cut me off because she knew exactly where my mind was.

I thought giving lil' mama some candy would keep her occupied long enough for me to lay and play between Niq's legs and make her gush right quick, but a nigga underestimated how fast the sugar was gonna kick in. Not even 10 minutes after I hit the door and slid baby girl the candy, she was runnin' wild and all up in me and Niq's mix, so I had to settle for some quick shower sex— quick because Essence was banging on the door before I even got a chance to dig Niq's walls out. She got some mind-blowing dome, and I got to finish off with a cold shower to douse my wood so my dick wouldn't enter the room before the rest of me. Just replaying that lil' shower scene had my shit tryin' to brick up, but thankfully, these arctic winds were right on time and made my manhood shrink back into place.

"Aight, ma. Put lil' mama to bed and get some rest." I ended the call so I could focus on makin' sure my Black ass didn't turn into a damn popsicle.

Pops always told me that in business, a man was only as strong as the support he had at home. Moms had been that strength for him for 28 years, and though I couldn't stand when a muthafucka started that *mama's boy* shit with me, I knew my future wife would be that same kinda strength for me. I was expecting Aniqa to pop the fuck off and make a nigga feel like shit for having to leave her and baby girl at the last minute, but she surprised me and gave me the green light to handle my business. I had already planned to do something nice for her, but seeing the way she was ridin' for me made me wanna go above and beyond to put a big ass smile on her face, so I made a note to set some shit in motion once I got back to VA.

My sweats weren't doin' a damn thing to ward off the chill, so I speed-walked and finally stepped foot inside the terminal. The warmth instantly went to work at raising my body temp back to a normal level, and just as I was shifting my carry-on bag to tuck my phone away, it started vibrating in my hand.

"Yo," I spoke, now balancing the phone between my cheek and shoulder as I fumbled with my bag.

"Dawg, you good?" Savage laughed; this fool stayed clowning.

"Nigga, what you think? It's cold as fuck out this bitch!" I snapped, making my way back to the exit.

Thankfully, the driver was there waiting with a sign that bore my last name. Judging by the way his cheeks and nose were beet red, he was just as underdressed as I was. I nodded my acknowledgement and he sprang into action, no doubt rushing to get back into the warmth of the chauffeured shelter from this harsh ass Denver night air. He opened the back door for me, but I waved him away and nodded for him to get back inside. Cold as it was outside, I wanted to finish my call with Savage before I got into the truck and had an audience. I didn't know the driver and as far as I was concerned, he was just as suspect as the rest of the names on my list, so I wasn't about to take a chance and have him ear-hustling on my end of the phone call.

"What's the move, though, bruh?" Savage probed.

I spent most of the flight out here thinking about the whole reason I had to make a trip out here in the first place. So much shit had been poppin' up and off, and since we could just about guarantee that the law was still watching Pops, it was more important than ever to shake out the weak links, tie up any loose ends, and quiet anyone that stood to put our shit at risk.

"Man, at first I was gon' just crash at Mique's spot, but it's still early as fuck and I'm thinkin' that element of surprise might work wonders for a nigga right now," I explained, shifting my weight from one foot to the other as I took a few steps away from the truck, making sure I was beyond the driver's earshot.

"Good shit," Savage agreed. "You already know I'mma

handle things out this way, so hit me if you need anything. I'mma run that other shit down and put you on once I know something."

"Bet. Get at me." I ended our call and rushed back over to the truck. The heat was blowing full blast and felt like heaven once I got situated in the back seat.

I ran down the name of the hotel I'd made a quick reservation at to the driver, then got comfortable for what I hoped would be a quick ride. The roads were empty, but I could see a fresh blanket of snow on the road as we exited the airport. I didn't know shit about driving in the snow, so I hoped this driver's skills were on point and he got my ass to The Westin in one piece.

I felt like I'd just closed my eyes when my phone started chiming per the alarm I'd set before I finally laid down. I knew my sister, LaMique, usually arrived at the dispensary a few minutes after opening, which was 9 a.m., but I had other plans for her today. I wanted to pull up on her before she even left the house this morning, so I willed my body to rise and get moving. I figured Niq was probably asleep by the time I made it to my suite, so I just shot her a text letting her know I was good and would hit her when I woke up. Checking my phone, I saw that she'd replied with a short video of her and baby girl clowning.

I swear Aniqa and Essence were my heart, and it was crazy because in the past, I didn't hesitate to curve a chick with kids. I didn't have time to play tug of war with the next nigga because he was in his feelings about another man bein' around his seed, so I just avoided it altogether. It was different with Niq, though, and if I was honest, baby girl won my heart over long before Aniqa did.

I called down to the front desk to let them know I was headed out shortly, and the attendant assured me she'd have my rental ready by the time I came down. Satisfied, I slid my phone back onto the nightstand and headed into the massive bathroom to shower the jetlag funk away; I didn't have the energy to do shit but slip on some shorts and climb into bed when I got in earlier.

A hot shower, some hot coffee, and a quick bowl of oatmeal later, I was in my rental and headed to my sister's spot. The roads were clear for it to have just snowed hours earlier, so I hoped I made it out to Mique's spot without sliding off the road and winding up in a ditch somewhere. I caught that show *Man vs. Wild* from time to time, but a nigga wasn't tryin' to live that shit in real life!

"Incoming call from..."

Just like I figured she would, Niq hit my line before I got

too deep off into my morning, but I was missing her lil' short ass anyway, so it was perfect timing. I glanced down the road and saw that traffic had slowed to a stop because of a lane closure, so Niq's call could keep my mind occupied during the stalled traffic as well.

"Yo," I spoke once the call was connected.

"And why–"

"I got you, ma. Haven't even had my eyes open for a good hour and I had to get right on the road to handle some business," I cut her off before she could even get started whining real good.

"Hmm, I guesssss I'll let that slide, but hold on. Someone wants to talk to you," Niq replied, and the line went quiet before my lil' sunshine's voice filled the interior of my rental.

"Heh-woooooo?"

"Hey short stack, whatcha doin'?"

"Weah you go?" Essence asked, and I could see her lil' eyebrows furrowed as though she was sitting right next to me.

"I gotta work, baby girl, but can you do me a favor?" I smiled.

"Huh?"

"Go get my homie Rumpy dressed so we can go see Chuck E."

"Yayyyyyy, Chuck E! We go see Chuck E!" she squealed as the sound of her voice faded off into the background.

"You know damn well you're not anywhere close to being home and able to take her to Chuck E. Cheese's. Why are you getting her hopes up like that?" Niq sighed as she came back on the line.

"You right, but you are, so make sure my princess gets up with that nigga Chuck E. today," I chuckled.

"Ugh, you make me sick!"

"No doubt, but you know you love a nigga. Check it, though..." I began, bracing myself for Niq's reaction because I felt in my gut she was about to turn up when I spoke my next words.

"Please don't be making any more damn plans for my day. I have enough to do today as it is, and I already know if I don't cash the check that your mouth just wrote, I'm gonna have to deal with a tantrum later on. Now, what's up?"

"Hold up— you gotta promise you gon' lemme finish AND that you gon' keep an open mind," I proposed.

"See, I knew you were about to come with some BS. I'm

not promising anything, so just go on and tell me."

Again, another eyeroll I couldn't see, but knew she had just sent through the phone.

"Look, we both know you ain't goin' nowhere anytime soon, and you damn sure ain't goin' nowhere with baby girl, so we gotta take this family shit seriously, feel me?"

"Okaaaaay, I thought we were already doing that..."

"Calm down, killa," I joked. I knew I needed to lighten the mood because I could already hear Aniqa getting defensive. "We are, but you know I ain't with half-doin' shit, so we gotta do this family thing right. I want us to sit down and give dinner with my parents another try–"

"Hell no, and you must be smoking some of that fruity ass weed y'all sell out there because you were wrong for even coming at me with that, Linc. What the hell?"

"Niq, chill. You ain't even think about it–"

"Don't need to. Neither me nor Essie is going anywhere near your mother until she apologizes for treating me like I was a musty pair of leggings," Niq cut me off, and I had to laugh at her dramatics.

"The fuck some musty leggings gotta do with this? You wild, yo."

"I'm not for it, Linc. Not gonna happen."

"Bae, think about what you said; how is Moms gonna have a chance to apologize if you won't even sit down with her?"

"Tell her to drop it in my DM because I refuse to deal with her, Linc, and how can you even expect me to after the way she acted?"

"Niq, baby, we gotta get past it at some point. I'm just asking you to do your part."

"How the hell do I have a part to do? I did my part by showing up last time and by being respectful in your parent's home, even though I wanted to slap fire from her!" Niq shouted.

"Whoa, chill on all that; ain't nobody doin' no slapping. I know you're upset and all, but that's still my mom. I respect yours, so respect mine."

"Are you serious? You wanna talk about respect? For real, Linc? How the f—"

"Ay, lemme hit you back." I ended the call more abruptly than I intended, but shit, my eyes had to be deceiving me.

I had just turned into the subdivision and down Canyon Rim Circle, the road that turned into a cul-de-sac where Pops had bought Mique a plush ass condo, but I didn't even get a good 20 feet down the road before I was hitting the brakes and pulling over to the side. I couldn't even see the cul-de-sac for the swarm of police cars that had set up a makeshift blockade, preventing any vehicles from venturing into the span of circular pavement that hugged the units at the end of the block, including Mique's.

The fuck?!

I gave a quick glance to take the entire scene in, honing in on where there seemed to be the most movement and greatest number of personnel– right at the foot of the steps that led up to Mique's front door. Now, what the fuck was really going on? Me and Pops took care to make sure Mique only touched the legit side of our business operations, and we mostly kept her name outta shit, so I was drawing a blank as to why the fuck what appeared to be Greenwood Village, Colorado's finest was posted up at her shit.

I sat there for a few more minutes and after looking even closer, I was sure that it was not only local law enforcement, but also the Colorado Bureau of Investigation (CBI) that was making fresh tracks in the snow, moving back and forth between Mique's front door and their group of vehicles.

Reaching over to open the glove compartment, I snatched up the burner I picked up just for this trip. After tapping out Mique's number, I was met with four long rings before her voicemail picked up. I couldn't see whether or not she was being detained in the back of one of the vehicles, and the absence of an ambulance had me feeling like the CBI's presence there definitely wasn't just a response to some sort of medical emergency. Still, I knew better than to assume that my sister had been in her place when they showed up, so I needed to pinpoint her location ASAP.

I tried Mique's number one more time and getting her voicemail yet again, I returned the phone to the glove compartment and slid my main phone out to hit my right-hand. My gut told me that all this police presence at my sister's spot was some ill shit, and the last thing we all needed was to be blindsided by more bullshit. I'd move better with my ace by my side, but shit, we'd just have to make it do what it do on some long-distance teamwork.

Chapter Two

Aniqa

My leg was bouncing so fast that you would have mistaken me for a marathon runner had I not been seated on the couch with my feet tucked under my thighs. It had been a good hour since Linc hung up in my ear, and I was still waiting for that *woosah* of calm to kick in; so far, it had failed me.

Linc hadn't been in Colorado long enough for the cold temperatures to put his brain cells on frigid, but something was definitely off up in his head if he thought for a second that I'd agree to break bread with his overbearing mother. Then, on top of that, his ass had the nerve to hang up in my ear just as I was about to get good and turned up with him? No bueno. I just couldn't seem to catch a break in the momma department, and though I didn't think anyone could be as bad as Je'Marcus' mother, Shirlene, Linc's mother was looking like a close runner-up.

Guess that's what I get for chasing mama's boys, huh?

That peace and calm was still a no-show, and I could feel my pulse racing at Nascar-speed, just thumping away in my temples as I called myself balancing my MacBook in my lap. I willed my eyes to focus on the blinking cursor, which was the only thing populating a barren *Page One* in my document, but I just couldn't do it; my mind was beyond gone. There was just no way I planned to suffer through another dinner with Linc's disrespectful ass mama.

Sighing deeply, I internally chastised myself to get back to where I knew my attention needed to be directed– this introductory essay that I should have been doing a final review of, but had yet to start the initial rough draft for. It was due in a few days, which meant I needed to get it submitted to turnitin.com tonight to make sure I had enough time to handle any last-minute tweaks. I had no motivation whatsoever to get it done, though. Despite my lack of interest, it was a requirement for my full admission to the Pre-Pharmacy program at HU, and knowing that I skated through and got admitted on a hope and a prayer, I had no room to mess up. I tried to shake off the irritation Linc had just dropped into my day and get back to brainstorming how I was going to put my own personal spin on methane hydrates– make no mistake, I was still mad as hell at the fight I'd just had with Linc, though.

It wasn't that Linc was being unreasonable in asking me

to give his mother another chance, and I knew that I couldn't really expect him to just cut his mama off because we got off on the wrong foot. He was just trying to do this whole kumbaya thing way too soon. His mother's antics were still throbbing as fresh bruises on my ego, and I was far from being in a forgiving mood. Besides, it wouldn't hurt for her to reach out on her own and offer me an apology before I just waltzed back up into the woman's house.

DING DONG!

Essence was still occupied back in her room— trying to find something for her lil' teddy bear to wear, per Linc's request— and the last thing I needed was another interruption or distraction, but that's exactly what the doorbell had just dealt to me. I guess I wasn't moving fast enough because whomever my unannounced visitor was decided to lean on the damn bell, filling the spacious loft that had become partly mine with its cheerful chime.

I'll be damned if I didn't speak too soon about Essie giving me a break because as soon as I blinked, I could hear her little feet padding down the hall as she scampered to the front door with excitement, anxious to see who had decided to pay us a visit. Her hands shot toward the door handle until she heard me clearing my throat behind her. Those big, beautiful brown eyes jumped up to meet mine as she stopped dead in her tracks. Swinging the door open, an ear-piercing excitement fell from Essie's mouth as she reached out for TJ like she hadn't seen him in years. Those two were really something else together, but I loved that they were toddler besties.

"Damn girl, what the hell took you so long? Thought I was gonna have to break the damn door down and make sure you and my baby were okay– what y'all got to drink up in here? I know Linc's uptown ass has some expensive liquor in there somewhere," Beautiful rushed, all in one breath, as she invited herself in and glanced over in the direction of the kitchen.

"Hey TJ, what's up, lil' handsome?" I spoke as I closed the front door.

"I got fake people sowin' fake wuv to me, stwaight up to my faaaaaaaace!" TJ burst out, and all I could do was laugh; his brow was furrowed and he used his hands to emphasize his words, so you could tell he was really feeling himself. His little behind really did think he was a mini-Drake!

I leaned down and gave TJ a quick peck on the forehead before he turned his attention back to Essence, then I stopped and paused for a second, looking up to the ceiling like there was a hidden message written in invisible ink. I loved my girl Bee to death, but I wasn't sure if I could take a super-sized dose of her dramatics today– and she was definitely on ten.

Lawd, give me strength.

"Oh Lord, do I even wanna know what's got you ready to drink this early in the day?" I smirked. "Wine is all I have, so it's gonna have to be good enough for now," I called over my shoulder as I dug around in the fridge to see what sort of libation I had to sate her thirst. Bee gave me a quick nod from the living room before she turned her attention to her goddaughter.

"Excuse me, lil' princess. Where's my love?" Beautiful called after Essence, who had already proceeded to drag TJ back to the playroom Linc had set up for her.

Turning around with the most adorable smile she could muster, she hurried into Beautiful's arms as a loving giggle escaped her chest. Shaking my head at the two of them, I went back to playing hostess, grabbing two glasses and a bottle of Chenin Blanc. I wasn't much of a liquor drinker anyway, and given the day I'd had so far, wine was just what the doctor ordered. My irritation with Linc was still lingering, and I needed something good to knock that edge off.

"What are you all dressed up for today?" I asked Beautiful, giving her a head-to-toe glance as I headed back to join her on the couch. Seeing Beautiful at her best wasn't abnormal, but I loved giving her high-maintenance ass flack.

"Girl, bye!" She dismissed me with a wave of her hand, brushing her wild curls back away from her face.

I had to wonder how many dudes Bee cursed out on her way over, which was how she handled any guy that tried to push up on her. I knew there was no way she made it all the way over here without making a few niggas' eyes pop out of the sockets, especially with the way the thickness of her curves was popping today. Beautiful knew she was thicker than a triple-thick milkshake!

I gave her outfit an awe-struck glance, taking in the skinny jeans that made her look like she'd been dipped and wrapped in denim. The asymmetric, flowing blouse that she wore was a perfect fit for her wild personality, and the way it showed just enough of her midriff to make you wonder how long it took her to get into her jeans spoke volumes of her self-assurance.

One of the main things I loved about Bee was her confidence; she embraced every inch of her curvy thickness, and she'd light your ass up for doing anything less than appreciating her beauty. The knee-high stiletto boots set the outfit off, though, and I made a note to ask her where she got them so I could snag myself a pair.

Add a flawless face-beat, and Beautiful stood there an accurate embodiment of her name; this chick looked like she was headed to an A-list, red carpet photo shoot! I thought it was a bit cool outside to have a cropped shirt on, but I decided to leave it alone because I just didn't have the energy to go back and forth with her; besides, she was grown.

"Unt uh— I know you ain't just slide over here with no cheap ass wine, girl. You ain't broke no more!" Beautiful boomed as I set the bottle and glasses down on the sofa table. "Don't nobody drink that generic shit!"

"And you passed how many stores on your way here? Oh, okay," I dismissed her little fit; this girl was really on one today! "So, spill it— what's got your ass all thirsty for a drink? I hope this isn't all behind Savage and that other chick," I picked her brain, filling both of our glasses and sitting back into the corner of the couch with my feet tucked under myself once again. She got over her little bougie moment real quick and happily raised her glass to her lips, swirling it around like they'd taught us to do at the wine-tasting event we attended a few months back.

Beautiful let out a long sigh after she took her first sip, and I could see all over her face that she had plenty of tea to spill, but before she could get a word out and bring me up to speed, her phone vibrated on top of her thigh. She looked down to check the display and groaned. Rolling her eyes at whoever was calling, she hit the green talk button. I could hear an automated voice blaring through and figured that the caller was Tyleek, little TJ's daddy.

"Yes," Bee responded to the robotic voice. Wanting to give her some privacy, I grabbed my phone and wine, then made my way back to the kitchen to busy myself with putting away the items in the dishrack I'd left out to air-dry after washing the dishes earlier. As usual, my mind came to rest on Linc, and I suddenly felt remorse for flipping out the way I had.

ME: *I'm sorry*

I shot him a quick text and sighed. I appreciated everything about Linc, and the last thing I wanted was for him to think I wasn't committed to making things work between us, especially given the way he accepted Essie right from the start and spoiled her like she was his own. Good men who prioritized taking care of home were hard to find; I knew that all too well considering how much hell Je'Marcus took me through over the years. Truth was, me and Linc's and I's relationship had been rocky from the start, but having placed so many obstacles behind us, I was looking forward to being with him— minus all the drama we seemed to inevitably attract.

"Hell no, Leek! And until you get that through yo' thick ass, nappy ass, ugly ass, dry-rotted ass head, don't call my fuckin' phone again!" I heard Bee yell. Tipping back into the living room, I could hear her mumbling under her breath about Leek getting on her damn nerves.

"You okay, girl?"

"Ouuuuuuuu, I swear that nigga makes my whole ass itch! He soooooo irks my soul, girl. Talkin' 'bout I need to get over myself and bring TJ up there to see him. That nigga done lost his mind and got me all the way fucked up!" she fussed.

Reclaiming my seat, I felt another shift in my emotions. Leek and TJ's relationship was always a touchy subject with Bee, so I erred on the side of peace and avoided it most times; I couldn't do that today, though.

"Beautiful, have you ever considered things from his perspective?" I quizzed, knowing my question would stir up an inferno of emotions in my friend. I readied myself as though I was bracing for some sort of massive impact.

"Excuse me?" she snapped, halting her glass midair on its way to her lips.

"Hear me out, now," I continued, laughing inside at how my words felt so similar to the ones Linc had just spoken earlier. "I'm just saying...TJ's a smart kid, and it's only a matter of time before he hits you with his own questions anyway, so how much longer do you plan on keeping the truth about his daddy from him?"

"As long as I feel the fuck like it," she checked me, cutting her eyes at me over the rim of her glass.

Leek would always be a sore subject, but fuck it, I had a little fire in me to go toe to toe with her now that the wine was kicking in, and I wasn't afraid to tread in deep waters when it came to Beautiful. We were like sisters in every sense of the word, and just like sisters had their differences, we were no exception.

"Essence asked about her daddy today," I spilled, revealing the real reason for my erratic jitters.

True, Linc's bright idea about another dinner with his parents had pissed me off, but it more so aggravated the foul mood I was already in carrying the mental burden of Essie's questions. "To be honest, I thought she meant Linc at first, but then I realized she was talking about Marcus."

"What'd you tell her?" Bee chugged her wine down and then reached for the neck of the bottle to pour herself a refill.

"Honestly Bee, I didn't know what to do. I mean, do I tell her she's never gonna see him again? And then what happens when she grows up and wants to know why she'll never see him again?"

All the frustration I had fought to put to rest came rushing right back to the surface. I knew Linc was doing what he thought was best for me and Essence, but he was still brand new to playing the role of a parental figure. He didn't understand that when there was a child involved, shit had to be handled differently; you couldn't just act on impulse and worry about the consequences later— you had to weigh those consequences on the front end. This wasn't just some random nigga that he'd decided to take out; it was my daughter's father, a man she would inevitably have a ton of questions about one day, and I would be forever stuck in the position of either lying to her by withholding what I knew, or telling her the truth and risking her having ill feelings toward me. Either way, neither of those were options I was looking forward to dealing with.

"Mama told me that TJ had asked her about his father too. Kids do that sometimes, but trust me girl, you're looking way too deep into this thing. Sometimes, we gotta do things we don't want to do, but it's in our kids' best interest to do so." She exhaled, and I felt like she was insinuating that my complaints were invalid or something.

"Yeah, but it's my job as her mother to always make the best possible decisions..."

"And you're doing that, Aniqa," she rebutted, her tone elevating a notch. "Look, I know you feel some type of way toward Linc for what he did to ol' bum ass, but damn, that shit was long overdue," she continued, emptying her second glass of wine. "It's like you have a good thing and still you don't appreciate this man for changing your life. Do you know how many times I stayed up late at night, wondering if this was the night I might get a call that Je'Marcus had finally succeeded at snatching the life out of your lil' ass? I worried about you more than I did my own damn self, but you know what I did out of love for your lil' ass? Played my part as your friend in the hopes that one day, you would wake up and see him for the fuckboy he really was, and you'd finally find your inner thug and leave his ass."

Just hearing her give me the CliffsNotes version of me and Je'Marcus' dysfunction reminded me of all the pain someone I once believed was the love of my life had taken me through. I tried to form at least a few words to respond to Bee and defend myself, but I got choked up and just opted to remain quiet and pull myself together.

"Fuck all that shit about him being E's daddy, so what? That nigga was never a daddy— he was a fuckin' donor. He lived foul, treated you like shit, and got exactly what the fuck his ass deserved. I, for one, don't feel bad at all and you know why? I can finally get a good night's sleep knowing that muthafucka will never lay his hands on you again."

Again, silence from me as a pool of tears clung to the

rims of my eyelids.

"Niq, you know just as well as I do that his ass was not gonna let you live in peace. His ass would've kept right on playing that *I Am King* role until your ass was six feet under. Shit, you oughta be thankful Linc put him down first."

Finally ending her tirade, Beautiful's face was contorted with disgust, and she looked utterly frustrated that I didn't share her sentiments.

"And you should be thankful TJ's father is alive," I retorted. "You know you're wrong for keeping him away from Leek, especially since there are so many Black boys in this country now without daddies–"

"Hold up! Pause! This ain't got shit to do with me! Our situations are totally different, so I don't see how the fuck you think you can compare the two. Leek got himself locked up; that shit don't fall on me! There's no way in hell I'm about to take my baby up in that place to be searched like a damn convict, just so he can see his lying ass daddy. If he was so concerned about being a father, he would've kept his ass on the right side of the law, so you can miss me with that shit, Niq!" Her voice rose, indicating that she was pissed off. "Besides, you have more than enough on your own plate than to be worried about what's on mine," she reminded me.

"And I could say the same about you," I clapped back.

This was, by far, the most heated disagreement we'd ever had, and I was almost afraid to see where it would go, particularly since there was no voice of reason in the room to play referee.

Cutting her eyes over at me as if she'd been betrayed, I could see that I had hit a nerve with Beautiful. Shooting up from her seated position like someone had lit fire under her, she took deliberate steps toward the back of the loft where the kids were.

"TJ!" she called her son's name at the top of her lungs. Staying planted in my spot on the couch, my heart raced as I realized that I might've gone too far.

"Come on, TJ. Put your shoes on," she mumbled the moment he popped his cute little face into the hall.

"Why, Mommy? I don't wanna goooo..."

"Let's go, TJ. Now!" she demanded.

The tension in the loft was so thick that even Essence didn't refute Bee's decision to leave as she stood watching her godmother rush TJ along.

"Beautiful..." I called her name, figuring the least I could do was attempt to calm her down. She waved me off like I knew she would, though.

"Nah, you straight. You said what was on your mind, and I heard you loud and clear," she spat, almost dragging TJ out the front door. The sound of it slamming behind her left me feeling lower than I'd felt when she arrived.

I knew her feelings were hurt more than anything. I rarely spoke my mind when it came to Beautiful, and that because she was usually right, but not this time. I didn't care how terrible of a person Je'Marcus had been to me; I still felt responsible for the fact that my child would never get to make her own decision of whether or not she'd allow her father to be a part of her life.

Bee had every right to be upset with Leek about his actions and the decisions that earned him a lengthy stay behind the walls of the Virginia Department of Corrections, but her anger over all of that didn't give her the right to deny TJ a relationship with his father. The way I saw it, she knew what kind of person Tyleek was when she decided to get involved with him, so she could only get so mad about the whole situation.

Today had definitely been one for the books, and the sun hadn't even gone down yet. I set my wine glass next to the one Beautiful held just minutes earlier, pulled my knees up to my chest, and let my head fall in a fitful rest against them. I already had way too much going on to be fighting with my best friend. To make matters worse, my research paper was still nowhere near being finished and at this point, I didn't even have the drive to finish it.

"Mommy, I weady go see Chuck E!" Essie's voice broke the stifling silence.

Can I get a do-over, Lord?

Chapter Three

Beautiful

I don't know who in the fuck Ms. Perfect little Aniqa thought she was today, but she had the wrong bitch if she thought she was about to preach to me about what I needed to do with someone I gave birth to. As fucked up as her shit was for so long? Hell nah, I ain't the one— not today, and not ever! She lucks up and finally finds a decent dude to rock with, and all of a sudden, she's a damn expert on parenthood? Fuck outta here!

I'd blown through two stoplights on the way to my mom's house; that's just how upset I was. All I wanted to do was go home, pour a real drink instead of that soft shit Aniqa gave me, slip into a steaming hot bubble bath, and call it a night. Leave it up to my toddler to throw a wrench in those plans, though.

"Mommy, we here!" TJ beamed as we pulled up in front of my mother's house.

He left his backpack here yesterday, and the last thing I

wanted to do was hear him whining all night because he didn't have it. I released the buckle for his booster car seat and, like always, he dashed past me and rushed up onto my mom's front porch, rising onto his tiptoes to ring the doorbell that he was finally tall enough to reach. My mom pulled the door open just as I cleared the last step and came to stand behind TJ on the porch.

"Hey, my baby!" Mama shined as she pulled TJ into a hug like she hadn't just seen him less than 24 hours earlier. "Oh, are you too grown to speak?" she called after me as I brushed past her on my way into the house.

"Hey Mama, where's his bag?"

"Oh no. No ma'am, hold on one minute." Mama whipped around and looked in my direction. Making sure TJ was inside, she pulled the screen door shut and pushed the front door up, leaving it open just a crack.

"I don't know what has your tail on your shoulders, but no ma'am, not up in here. We don't do that. Now, if you want to talk about what's bothering you, talk. Otherwise, check that funky little attitude at the door," she scolded as she pointed toward the front door. Normally, I'd have my usual clap back primed and ready to go — although I always gave my mother a stripped-down version of it — but I didn't even feel like going there with her right now.

The truth of the matter was that I was mad at both Aniqa and myself; her for calling me out and speaking what I knew was the truth, and myself for being in the situation in the first place.

"Why yes, my day was fine, I'm feeling well— thanks for asking, daughter of mine," Mama mocked me. "You rushed in and out yesterday like a tornado, then you come storming back in here like someone stole your snack pack or something. I really need you to get yourself together, girl."

Wanna know one of the things I loved about my mom? Even in the worst of moods, she always managed to make me crack a smile, and with no effort at all.

"Ma, what in the world is a snack pack?" I grinned.

"It's that stash of junk food you know you're not supposed to have, but you keep it put to the side anyway like an emergency survival thing. You know," she called over her shoulder as she dug around in her coat closet for TJ's backpack.

"I'm glad you stopped back by, though. Saves me a phone call. You know my follow-up is next week, and I'll need you to go with me."

I instantly felt my insides lock up like I was constipated after eating Taco Bell for a week straight.

Khadra Mudarris had long been a hero in my book, but seeing the way she was handling her recent health issues? Man, my mom was my she-ro, and I couldn't imagine ever not having her around. After being diagnosed with breast cancer some months back, she'd undergone a double mastectomy and was doing a hell of a lot better than any of her doctors expected her to. Still, that C word was a very real threat since there was chance it could pop back up soon, and it was that *chance* that made me sick to my stomach anytime I thought about her diagnosis.

"Come on, now. Don't start that. Look, I feel good, and you can't tell me that I don't look good, honey!"

Mama twirled around right there next to the closet door. She was right, though. She looked damn good to be mother to a grown woman, and a grandmother as well.

"If you all are lucky and stop doing all this turning up that you young folks talk about, you and Aniqa MIGHT look this good when you get my age."

She winked and just that quickly, at the simple mention of my friend, my mood took a nosedive toward the sour end of the spectrum.

"Ohhh, so that's what your problem is. What do I always tell you? Sisters fight, but they get over it and move on, so take your little time out in your corner, and then you two better get it together and fix whatever it is."

"Bu–" I began, but she shut me down.

"Unt uh, I don't wanna hear it, don't wanna know what it's about. I just need to hear that you two fixed it like the mature, grown women and mothers that you are. Got it? Now, how's my grandbaby doing in school?" she switched the subject.

Before she got sick, Mama used to keep TJ during the day for me and was used to spending a lot of time with him. Once she got sick, though, I put him in preschool and she only saw him during the week when she would get him off the bus. It turned out to be a good move for TJ because he really needed to be socializing with other kids his age while learning all the things that would get him ready for kindergarten, but I knew Mama missed spending her days with him.

"Fine; the class clown, of course, but he's loving all the new friends he's making."

"I miss my little man so much during the day, but it's good for him to be developing those social skills and what not, so I'm glad to hear that. And what about you? You decided what you're going to do with yourself?"

Of course, this was going to come up. Before Mama got sick, I was just weeks away from entering the military and heading off for my initial training, but hearing that my mom had cancer just shifted something inside of me. All I could think about was what would happen if I was off somewhere in another country and she got sick or passed away before I could get home to her. That thought alone was enough to make me rethink my plans and come to the decision that I couldn't leave. So, here I was, determined to stick close to home so I could be here for my mother, but unsure of what my next move should be or what I was gonna do with my life.

"I guess I'll go to school or whatever," I mumbled, getting comfortable because I knew exactly where this conversation was going.

"Beautiful, that's your answer to too many questions lately. *It's whatever.* It can't just be whatever, baby. You have to be purposeful in all that you do; whether it's a big move or a small step, you should always strive to move with purpose. I feel like you default to college because you think that's what you're supposed to do now that you've decided not to go into the military. Don't get me wrong, you know I'm all for education, but is that really what you want to do?" Mama probed.

"I mean, what else is there?" I sighed, feeling that same frustration I always felt whenever I asked myself what I was doing with my life.

I knew one thing, though: I was not about to just sit back and be a baby mama and live off the child support payments that the state had no idea Leek was siphoning off to me. Try as they might, that was a piece of information that the state's attorney couldn't get him to divulge. Hell, even I didn't know where his stash was, nor just how much cash he'd managed to tuck away.

I also knew I wasn't about to sit back and play sister wife to whoever this chick was that Savage had waiting in the wings on pause all this time.

"That's something you'll have to do, honey— find out what else is out there for you. Just do it soon because it's not a good look for you to be sitting next to TJ in English 101," Mama teased, bringing me to a much-needed laugh yet again.

"I see you got jokes, huh?"

"Always, honey. Now, what is going on with this visitation thing with Tyleek and TJ?"

And there it was— the very thing that I wanted to just forget about today. Damn, why was my baby daddy's name in everybody's mouth today?

"Mom, I don't wanna discuss Leek or that situation right now."

"That's not what I asked you– I asked you what was going on with that *situation*."

"And I said I don't want to talk about it, Ma. Can you just leave it alone?" I begged.

"So, leave the fact that my grandbaby is inquisitive alone. Leave the fact that he has questions about where he came from alone..."

"Mom, I plan to do everything I can to make sure that boy never sees the inside of anybody's detention, jail, or prison, so I'm not about to subject him to that!" I snapped.

"Subject him to what? Getting to meet his father? Building a relationship with the man? I'm sorry, I missed the part where that's somehow detrimental to TJ's well-being," Mama asserted, standing her ground.

"So, you think it's appropriate for him to be frisked and searched, to have to pass through whatever sort of clearance process they have before they let you in to visit?"

"And you think it's appropriate that he grow up not knowing who his father is? Beautiful, you did not make him alone, and as long as that man wants to be a part of his son's life, no matter how limited that involvement might be, you don't have a right to rob TJ of that experience. You do that and you're no better than these other bitter young girls that think their kids are pawns in some kind of game, and that they're punishing the child's father by not allowing him to see the child. I didn't raise you to be bitter or vindictive."

"You didn't raise me to be a fool either, did you?" I shot back.

"You're right about that, but clearly you don't always listen to me, now do you?"

"And that's my cue— let's go, TJ! We'll get that damn bag later!"

"Watch your mouth in my house, little girl!"

"TJ, NOW!" I summoned my son in a fit of rage for the second time today.

TJ knew me well enough to know when he could try me and get away with it, and he knew now was not one of those times, so he quietly made his way over to my mom to get his hug.

"Bye, baby. Come see me tomorrow, okay?" Mama bent down to hug him again, taking one last shot at me. She knew damn well I wasn't about to bring my ass over here tomorrow with the way she'd just pissed me off.

"Bye, Nana," my son uttered, head hanging low as she walked him over to the front door. I didn't speak; I didn't have a damn thing to be cordial about, so I opted to keep my mouth shut to keep from sliding into the disrespectful tirade that I really wanted to unleash on my mother.

"Mmm hmm, and I still love your mean behind. Get yourself together, daughter," Mama yelled as I stomped off to my car once we were out the door.

TJ was knocked out by the time I was merging onto the highway, so I spent the quiet ride home thinking about all the unsolicited advice that people seemed so quick to send my way today. I knew this issue would come up; I just wasn't ready to deal with it. TJ was hell on wheels when he was going through those terrible two's, and I felt like I was just getting to a point where I could enjoy him again and not feel like I spent all day trying to correct and reprimand him.

I loved my baby boy to death, and I liked the little life I had started to build for us. He was a good kid with the sort of infectious laughter and personality that you couldn't help but fall in love with, and I was afraid of having that all undone if I allowed him to visit with Leek. I'd done my share of reading on how to co-parent when the other parent is incarcerated, and I kept reading how even being in that sort of environment could kick off behavioral issues with kids, and I just didn't want to deal with all that. Still, I had to wonder if I'd really be able to pull off raising TJ all the way to high school graduation without letting him see or get to know his father.

Done with all this bullshit for the time being, I exited the highway and drove the short distance down to my apartment complex, and wouldn't you know it? Savage's ass was parked in my guest spot and awaiting my arrival. This nigga was the last person I wanted to see right now, and since I couldn't curse my mama out, he was about to be the unlucky recipient of a big helping of my frustration— starting now!

"You got some fuckin' elephant balls and alotta nerve bringing your ass over here— you lucky my baby's in the car 'cause I should fuck your ass up for even thinking you were about to play me to the left like some fuckin' jump off!"

I jumped out of the car the minute it was in park and charged in his direction.

"Ma, if you don't chill with all that noise; ain't nobody scared of yo' ass, and I ain't worried about you doing shit but opening that door and taking yo' ass inside before you let these neighbors know how crazy yo' ass really is." Savage chuckled, completely unfazed by me.

"These muthafuckas BEEN knew how crazy I was, but they're smart enough to know when the fuck to stay away from my ass— unlike you! Get the fuck out my way, boy!" I barked, trying to move past him and get to my back door to get TJ into the house. Thankfully, he was still knocked out and oblivious to me and Savage's exchange.

"Move, girl." Savage gave me a gentle shove.

"I said get out my way!"

"Man, if you don't gon' somewhere with that shit. Move so I can get lil' man in the house 'cause you clearly on some other shit. Fall back, now," Savage asserted, maintaining his stance while he summoned a little extra bass and called himself checking my ass. I ain't gon' lie– that shit had me turned the fuck on, so you know what I did, right? Moved the fuck out the way!

Chapter Four

Savage

I couldn't front; Beautiful had really gotten under a nigga's skin, and I had mad love for her evil ass. Actually, it was deeper than that— I think I was really *in love* with her. I just didn't know if I was ready for that kinda love. I wasn't about to tell her that, though.

"Man, if you don't get your ass over here," I teased, doing my best to keep from laughin' in her face.

I had just stepped back into her living room after layin' lil' man down in his bed, and her mean ass had gone above and beyond to move clear across the room to the other end of the sofa. I knew she was mad, and not that she didn't have a reason to be, but she needed to kill the dramatics.

"Man, if you don't get your ass the fuck up out my shit!" she snapped back. "I told your ass from jump that I wasn't with the games. You remember what you told me? *I ain't on that shit, Bee. You ain't gotta worry, Bee.*"

"And I meant what I said too." I smirked, walking over to sit right next to her because she knew damn well she wanted a nigga up in her face.

"And I meant it when I said all I wanna do is fuck. YOU were the one that wanted to be on some *boo* and *bae* shit."

True shit, and definitely one of the things that threw me for a loop about Beautiful's wild ass. Where most females were plottin' on how to trick a nigga into a relationship after a cheap ass trip through the drive-thru, Bee let me know from jump I could dick her down and never call back, and she wouldn't trip. Every man's dream, right? Now, I normally would've taken her up on her offer, but something just wouldn't let me walk away from her ass. Emani was the last chick I kicked it with that made me wanna do more than just fuck, and not that Bee was a replacement for Mani, but she definitely had a nigga looking forward to the next time she decided to cuss me out over some silly shit. Dysfunctional, yes, but it made a nigga's dick brick up every damn time.

"How you figure I'm playin' games, tho?" I pressed, wanting to see what she was really upset about. Was she mad because I dipped out on her, or was she mad because she thought I was with another bitch?

"I'm not about to do this with you— bye, get out my shit!" she snapped again, jumping up to her feet and attempting to

68

stomp over to her front door. I caught her arm before she could get too deep into her stride, though, and pulled her back down over to me.

"C'mere," I whispered.

"Fuck no, and let me go."

"Ma, just come sit down. I gotta show you somethin' right quick."

"Oh yeah, you can show me somethin'– your simple ass on the other side of my door, now step!"

She pulled back against my grip and turned like she was gonna head toward the door again, but I had other plans for her. Waiting for her to ease up on her lean, I jerked her forward in my direction and in a seamless motion, grabbed her body up, got to my feet, thrust her back down against the couch, and tore her jeans away so I could shut her ass up for the night.

"Stoooooop..." she fake-protested.

Now, her mouth was saying stop, but the way her legs spread without coercion let me know what was really up.

Slipping her legs into the crooks of my arms, I pulled her thick ass to the edge of the couch and got comfortable on my knees. Beautiful's thickness defied description, and I figured it had to be because of all that sweet, sugary gushiness that her walls were about to spray me with. It had been more than a few days since we got up, so I knew she'd probably wet me up with a tsunami before I made her tap out, and a nigga was all for it!

"Mmm, you know what I want, baby?" Beautiful cooed, sucking her juicy ass bottom lip between her teeth; with the way she scrunched her face up like she was already two seconds away from exploding, I just knew she was about to hit a nigga with some extra freaky shit.

"What you want, ma?" I whispered, gently tugging her clit between my teeth.

"To know what the fuck you had better to do the other night than break bread with me like you promised."

Just that quick, Bee went from hot to cold, and I could tell from the look on her face that there was about to be some shit. Of course, I knew what she was thinking, but I wasn't tryin' to argue with this girl. Fuck all that— I was trying to make up by diggin' her walls out.

"What you talkin' bout, ma?"

The look on my face said I was confused, but I could see she wasn't buying that shit.

"Oh, you slow now? WHERE *clap* THE *clap* FUCK

clap WERE *clap* YOU?"

She mashed her hand into the top of my head to keep me from finishing what she knew was guaranteed to make her forget why the fuck she called herself being mad.

"I told you, some shit came up, ma. I just needed to make a run and handle some shit."

"And I told you that sounded like some bullshit."

"Beautiful–"

"Nigga, answer my fuckin' question. Better yet, answer this: was your something that came up named Emani?"

You know how a female asks you a question that she already knows the answer to? How she gets that look on her face like she's daring you to let a lie even dance across your tongue? And how you beg your face not to give away the fact that you know she done caught your ass in some shit? Current situation.

"Why you on this again, Bee?"

"Why are you full of shit again, Sampson?"

"Oh word? You outta pocket, girl," I mumbled, shaking my head because it was a sure bet this shit was gonna end ugly since she was dropping my government.

"See, this is the reason why y'all niggas make me so fuckin' sick. I asked you for a simple yes or no, and you're actin' like it's a multiple-choice question and you need to phone a friend or some shit. Yes or no— were you with the bitch? It's real simple."

She was still in the same position with her legs spread open, teasing me with some shit she wasn't even tryin' to let me sample tonight. I kept trying to ease back up into her space and suck her into a coma, but she muffed the fuck outta me each time.

"Why you ask shit you know you don't wanna know the answer to? If I say no, I'm a fuckin' lie. If I say yes, I'm a sorry muthafucka. Either way, you know yo' ass don't wanna hear the answer, so let that shit ride. Better yet, ride this dick."

She had eased back up into a seated position, so I jerked her ass back down to the edge of the couch. Just when it looked like she was about to give in and let me get in, she hauled off and slapped next week's taste from a nigga's mouth.

"On some real shit, you need to chill the fuck out!" I roared, reeling back and jumping to my feet. She popped a nigga so hard it brought tears to my eyes, and that shit had me heated. I didn't put my hands on females, but I swear she was tryin' to see how far she could push ya boy.

"I told you, I'm not about to play house with a nigga that's in love with the next bitch, but I see you think I'm fuckin' playin'. But check it— see your way the fuck up out my shit, and lose my fuckin' number!"

Beautiful jumped up, ass and pussy still out, and pushed me toward the door.

"Don't put ya fuckin' hands on me, girl."

"Nigga, you ain't 'bout to do shit but stand there and look like the liar you are. Get the fuck OUT!"

"Man, you on stay on some bullshit."

"And do— bye, nigga!"

It felt like she pushed me as hard as she could until I had tripped over her threshold and onto her doorstep. Thankfully, I had my keys in my pocket because the minute my feet cleared her door, she slammed and locked that muthafucka. I didn't even bother to turn around and look, or to hit her door and try to reason with her. Times like this, a nigga was so tempted to dip back and fuck with Emani since Bee's crazy ass swore that's what a nigga was doing anyway.

Back in my car, I put my shit on cruise control and just drove, not even thinking about where I was headed. On some real shit, I felt like my heart was torn between both Bee and Emani. This shit with Bee caught me off-guard because I had every intention of giving her what she wanted by keepin' it on some straight fuckin' shit between us. I had history with Emani, though, some history that was interrupted, so it was hard for me to just push her completely outta my mind. I loved Emani, and I knew she felt the same about me, but she made it clear she wasn't interested in tryin' to rekindle the past when I first got out. She said she'd love a nigga from a distance and leave it at that. On the other hand, if I was gonna try to do the relationship thing, Bee would probably be the one I'd give it a try with, but she didn't trust a nigga and that shit was frustrating. Normally, niggas stayed tryin' to convince a female they were doing right when they already had another bitch lined up to fuck. This time, I was tryin' to get my grown man on and maybe build some shit, but it was like she wanted me to be that nigga that would play with her head, put miles on her pussy, and keep it movin'.

LINC: *Nothing yet?*

My phone lit up with a text from my boy, Linc, just as I was switching lanes to leave the highway, so I shot him a quick reply. His message was a reminder that I had some business shit I needed to tend to, and stopping by to see Beautiful had thrown me all off track.

I guess Mani had a stronger hold on me than I realized because when I looked up, I was exiting the highway and turning into her neighborhood. The more I thought about it, the more I felt like maybe Bee saw something that I didn't realize was there, like maybe she could see that a nigga's heart wasn't done with Emani. How does a nigga get done with a female he never got the chance to fully love, though?

"I don't know how, but I knew you were gonna stop by tonight." She smiled when she opened the door. I must've really been on autopilot because I don't know when I parked my shit and made it to her front door. She stepped aside to let me in, and I could tell from the look on her face that she was really going through with her health.

"How you feelin'?" I helped her back to the oversized chair I could see that she'd been curled up in before I showed up.

"I'm makin' it."

She gave me a weak smile that tugged at my heart because I knew she had to be stressed out about her situation. "So, what brings you by? Because I know you didn't come all out the way for nothing."

"Honestly ma, I don't even know... I just wound up here."

"You know why that is, right?" Her voice sounded so weak and strained when she spoke.

"Nah, but I know you gon' run it down to me."

"Because there's something here you're supposed to have," she replied. I looked over at her and held her gaze for a good minute, just waiting to see what she was going to say next.

"Savage, I love Dre more than anything in this world, even myself. I know what I'm facing. I've accepted it, but I'd have a little more peace knowing that I'm leaving him with someone I know loves him," she began.

Emani was askin' me for something most biological fathers would feel overwhelmed with: to raise her son in the event that she passed away. I wasn't even ready to have kids of my own, so what the hell did I look like playin' daddy to her seed? I cared for lil' man; shit, even loved him because he was a part of her, but damn. This was a lot. I knew I could be a fucked-up nigga with some fucked up ways, and I might slip up and live foul from time to time, but how the fuck was I gonna be somebody's daddy right now?

"I know it's a lot, I get that, but we don't have anyone else, Savage."

Silence. I mean, I couldn't say shit. My mind was racing a million miles a minute.

"I know it has to be weird to talk about your new love with your old love, but I can see that you care a lot about her, Savage." She gave me another weak smile.

"I wouldn't say all that, ma."

"You don't have to. I can see it in the way you move. She's good for you, and you deserve to be happy. Just like Dre does. He's a kid, and all he knows is he wants to grow up and be a racecar driver. Can you help him make it there?" she pleaded, and I felt so fucked up. How could I tell her yes? If I did, I knew this shit with me and Bee was a wrap.

"Promise me that you will at least think about it?"

"I mean... I don't wanna disappoint you, Mani."

"As long as you love him like you loved me, you won't. Remember what we used to say? Got your back even in death?"

I dropped my head in a slow nod as I thought back to what me and Mani used to be. Even more than being afraid of the thought of having to care for her son, I think I was more scared of how it would feel to have to watch her being laid to a final resting place. That fear was quickly replaced by how Bee's wild ass would react if I did decide to move forward and raise Mani's lil' man once she was gone.

Damn, what was a nigga gon' do?

Chapter Five

Linc

Mique still wasn't answering her phone, but I didn't want to panic yet since it was possible she wasn't even home when the law showed up; not likely, but still possible. I still hadn't let Pops know what I rolled up on, and I planned to keep it on the low until I knew for sure what the deal was; I didn't want him to get upset and spun up over shit for no reason.

I decided to head over to the shop and surprise the staff by being there before anyone else arrived. I knew Mique had a manager that normally opened so she wouldn't have to be there first thing in the morning, and I wanted to see if anyone was especially shook by my presence. If everything was on the up and up, they had no reason to be worried, but Pops always said a hit dog will holler, so I wanted to see who might be the first to sound off.

ME: *Nothing yet?*

SAVAGE: *Nah, stay by ya phone tho*

Part of me was hoping I'd run into Mique when I got to the shop, but I found the parking lot covered in the fresh blanket of snow that was falling when I touched down hours earlier. The tracks left by my rental were the only disruption to the powdery sheet of precipitation– the only disruption except for the trail left by a car that was parked in a far corner of the parking lot.

The hell?

Carmichael Organic Therapy, our Colorado chain of dispensaries, was the only building tied to this lot. We owned the whole strip and used the adjacent spaces for storage and production, but there was plenty of parking right up front near the main entrance, which made the car look even more out of place tucked off in the corner. I killed the engine and the lights, then reclined my seat back a little more, giving myself a good vantage point to check out the driver of the other car without them being able to see me.

It was a few more minutes before the driver exited the other car, and after looking around to check their surroundings, the person's eyes came to rest on the rental I was driving. I still couldn't tell if the person was male or female, but they stood there for a good ten seconds staring at my rental. I saw the lights flash on their car, like they hit a button on a key fob to lock the doors, then the person stalked across the parking lot and passed not even a foot in front of the bumper of my rental. I saw the person cut a glance in my direction like they were trying to see if anyone was inside my vehicle, and that's when I saw exactly who this person was— Jason, the same funny-lookin' nigga that I suspected was working for the Feds. I got a strange vibe from this nigga the first time I laid eyes on him, and after Savage had him checked out and found that he didn't exist on paper beyond the past few years, this Jason cat was lookin' more and more like someone we needed to handle.

I watched him for the next few minutes as he made his way up the stairs, unlocked the entrance, and went inside. I sat there debating if I should run up in the shop and handle him before any of the other employees showed up, or if I should just sit back and see who else showed up next. Just when I was about to make a move, my main phone rang and pulled my attention away from the shop's entrance. Seeing that it was Mique finally returning my call, I jumped to answer the call.

"Yo, where the hell you at?" I spat.

"I had to go to the hospital, I wasn't feeling well. What the hell is wrong with you?"

"Hospital for what? Never mind, check it— meet me at the Westin out by Denver International."

I ended the call, looked at the entrance to my family's

business one more time, and then cranked the engine up so I could go and see what the fuck was really going on with my sister. I still wasn't sure how much she knew about all the shit Kappo was involved in; plus, I wanted to know why the fuck she was at the hospital.

"What are you doing here? And when did you get here? Why didn't you tell me you were coming?"

Mique was firing one question after another, but I shut her down. We had just stepped into my suite and she rushed past me to toss her purse and coat onto the sofa, then plopped down next to her pile of belongings like she'd been on her feet all day.

"Why is the law all over yo' shit? And what did yo' ass have to go to the hospital for?" I dropped my keys onto the coffee table and posted up right across from her, leaning against the wall so I was in her direct line of sight.

Mique and I had this unspoken animosity between us for as long as I could remember. She wasn't my favorite person, but I still loved her because she was my sister. I just hoped I could continue to *not* hate her and not be tempted to body her ass for being involved in this dirty ass plot that felt like Kappo was trying to set Pops up to take the fall for some snake shit. Everything in me told me she was involved in some kinda way, and the only reason she was free from bodily harm was because she was my sister. On the strength of that, I owed it to both Moms and Pops to give her a chance to clear her name.

"Hold on, what cops? I haven't been home since late last night..."

She was only half listening to me as she had quickly diverted her attention to her phone. Just that quick, she'd become engrossed in whatever was the source of the vibrating notification that had just come through– disrespectful and suspect as fuck, considering her crib was currently under siege.

"And why is that?" I pressed.

I could see her lil' attitude rising up, and I had to remind myself she was my sister because I really wanted to reach out and choke the shit outta her for being so nonchalant.

"None of your damn business– what the hell is going on? Why are you even here?"

"Why the fuck you been stealin' from Pops?"

I rushed up into her face, getting so close that she would inhale the frustrated breath I was about to release. I needed to see exactly what ran through her head as she processed my question, especially since it felt like she was being hella evasive.

"Mique, you better tell me somethin'!" I roared, snapping my sister's gaze away from whatever the fuck had her attention on her phone. I was fighting harder than I expected to calm the fire brewing inside since all this shit kicked off with the law coming after my pops.

"Shut up! Just shut up! I need quiet!" Mique shrieked, perplexing the shit outta me. Who the fuck did she think she was bassin' up at?

"Just shut up! I need to think!"

I put my interrogation on pause and just stood there, arms snapped tightly across my chest. I had to squeeze my biceps to keep myself from reaching out and touching her.

"Linc, I don't know anything about the cops being at my house, I can promise you that. I don't know what's going on, but I don't have the energy to do this with you right now," she breathed, teetering on the edge of a helpless plea.

"LaMique, all bullshit aside, posted up in a hotel room in the middle of a fuckin' blizzard with you is the last place I want to be, but there's some foul shit goin' on and if you don't have answers for me, I'm gon' just have to assume you're part of that same foul shit. So, what's it gon' be?"

The tone of my voice was icy cold, but the fire racing through my veins was anything but. Mique felt the shit too because she finally put her phone to the side and adjusted her posture to make it clear that I had her undivided attention.

"This nigga Megga that you begged Pops to rock with on this side business shit? The nigga is Kappo's cousin. Explain."

Mique had a chocolate complexion, but her face went ashen as those last few words fell from my lips. She froze right there on that couch, almost like she was a long-lost member of a flash mob that was waiting on her downstairs in the lobby. A good two minutes passed before she found her voice.

"Wha-how do you know—"

"Explain to me how the fuck you *didn't* know."

A deep scowl settled on her face, and knowing her the way I did, I guessed her mind was racing through several months of conversations, meetings, and random interactions she'd had with Kappo, trying to do a quick assessment to uncover any missed red flags she should have caught. It was too late now, though. The damage was done and it looked like Kappo's snake ass had succeeded at a deceitful larceny of not only Pops' trust, but also Mique's pussy. A trickle of tears sprung up and took turns racing down her cheeks as she displayed something I hadn't seen in years: sincere emotion.

"I swear I didn't know, Linc. I didn't know..." Her hand flew up to cover her mouth as a flash of realization skipped through her eyes.

"What?" I pressed.

"I-I just didn't know. I mean..."

"What do you and that nigga speak about when you're not fuckin'?"

The more I thought about it, the more I realized Kappo had shown his bitch nigga tendencies before, but we just never picked up on the shit because he was an expert at shifting the heat to make it look like other niggas were comin' up short. This nigga stood there with a straight face while Pops smoked Gino, his last right-hand, knowing full well it was behind some bogus shit and the nigga was innocent. That shit never sat right with me, so I knew it was possible that Kappo might've let some shit slip out while he called himself pillow talkin' with the boss's daughter.

"N-nothing really. He said he had some things in the works to take the business to the next level, but I just thought that meant Megga planned to up things on his end," Mique explained.

"How much does he know about the business out here? I know the nigga's been flyin' back and forth, and it wasn't for anything Pops told him to check into. How much did you tell him besides the surface shit?"

"Well, since we started...you know...he's been almost like another manager for me...off paper, of course. He had some good ideas to sort of improve our flow—"

"And this *improved flow* gave him access to what?"

I was the one frowning now because my hands were itching to slap some sense into my sister. She was far from a dumb chick, even borderline genius when it came to her craft; I'd give her that, which is why I couldn't understand how the fuck she got hustled by Kappo. Right now, she was the true definition of a chick that was dumb off the dick.

"So, with this new flow, who was responsible for the deposits?" I pressed since she acted like she didn't hear me the first time.

My gut told me the answer to this question, but I knew I couldn't go back to Pops with assumptions and gut feelings, especially with Mique being caught up in this shit. She still had him wrapped around her finger to an extent, and he'd never be quick to think the worst of her, so I needed some airtight proof before he'd see the role she played in all this: a piece of ass to let the next nigga get a leg up on how we did business.

Mique didn't offer a verbal response to my last question; she didn't need to because the repentant grimace of her face told it all.

I wasn't worried about Kappo personally fuckin' with anything else, but I was sure he had some help in all that he'd managed to slip past us, so I was concerned about who else we needed to make plans to handle.

"Oh God, Linc..."

"Too late to call on him now."

I felt like the more I asked Mique, the dumber she got. All I wanted to do was get shit back on track with the business, body whoever the fuck got in my way, and get the fuck up outta little Antarctica, so I needed her to get off the dumb blonde shit and get her mind right.

"Check it, how has this dude Jason been actin' and movin' lately?" I redirected our conversation.

"He's at work every day like he's supposed to be, even opens for me sometimes." Mique leaned over to grab some tissue from the coffee table and get her face together.

"Who opened for you today?"

"Jason, I believe— hold on, this is him calling me now."

Mique pulled her phone from her bag and took the call just as my own phone started jumping on my hip. Seeing that it was a call from Savage, I stepped into the bedroom portion of my suite and shut the door; I still didn't fully trust Mique to the point where I felt comfortable with her listening in on my conversations.

"Yo, what's good?" As always, Savage had a knack for calling right on time.

"Man, shit's crazy! I can't fuckin' win for losin'!"

I assumed he was referring to the shit between him and Beautiful. Despite all the crazy shit we had going on with business, I really wanted to see my boy find the kinda thing I found with Aniqa— even though that girl could be so stubborn that it made me wanna reach out and shake the shit outta her sometimes. There just seemed to be too many outside forces that were determined to pull Savage and Beautiful apart, though.

"What's the deal now, bruh?"

"Man, that shit at Mique's spot? My folks said a warrant came through early this morning after some anonymous tip was called in."

The fuck?

Anonymous my ass; everything in me said this Jason cat had something to do with it all. Before I could reply to Savage, we were interrupted by Mique's knock at the door.

"Bruh, I'mma hit your line right back."

Ending the call, I rejoined Mique in the living room area to see what was up.

"I need to get over to the shop and tend to a few things, are you coming with me?"

"Things like what? I need to kick some shit down to you about Jason."

"I need to go home first, but can we talk about it on the way over?"

"Did you not hear me when I said the law got your shit on lock?"

"I didn't do anything, though, Linc. I need to go home first."

"I can't let you do that, sis, not until we know how and why they're there. Lemme drive you to the shop, though. We need to talk about some shit on the way over anyway. Pops has some things he needs you to put into place before you go up in there today."

"What about my house? And the cops?"

Mique looked lost as fuck, like a little girl that had misplaced her doll or some shit. I almost felt sorry for her, but that shit passed quicker than a bitch spreads them legs once you put a ring on it.

"We're gonna handle that too. Just get your shit so we can go."

I kept right on moving past her as I spoke; didn't even look her in the face, just told her what she needed to do because quite frankly, I didn't have shit else to say to her. As far as I was concerned, it was her fault I had to fly out here in the first place, and I just wanted to get back home ASAP so I could fuck Niq's lil' attitude right on up out of her soul.

"Fine, let's just go," she huffed, snatching her bag and coat up in what I assumed was a muted tantrum. Just then, I remembered I had one more question I needed to ask her concerning all the events we'd been hit with lately.

"That bitch Tiara. Your damn soror and low-key bestie? How does she know Kappo?"

Mique threw me a puzzled look, like I was asking a question I should have already known the answer to.

"Kappo is her father."

What the fuck!

Chapter Six

Aniqa

ME: *Still mad?*

Peering down at my phone, I gave the message one last glance before I tapped the arrow and sent it through to its intended destination. I'd been sitting there staring at it for a good five minutes, unsure of whether I should send it or continue to maintain my stance. I didn't feel like I'd said anything wrong; if anything, I was the one that had a right to be all upset and in my feelings. I continued staring at the screen, hoping to see a notification that the message had been read, hoping to see those three little dots twerking in place to indicate that I had a response on the way. Sadly, neither of those occurred and as seconds grew into minutes, I realized I was probably being ignored.

Damn, Beautiful can really hold a damn grudge when she wants to!

"Mama! Mama!" Essence sang, attempting to snatch my

phone out of my hand.

"Stop!" I chastised with a bit more force than I intended to.

Beautiful and I were two days into what was probably the worst fight we'd had in all the years we had known each other. My legs bounced and my stomach swirled as I focused what was probably a little too much on the status of our message thread.

CRASH!

I shot up from my seat like I'd been shocked with a taser, stepping right into an unexpected rush of liquid that blessed the top of my feet and soaked the ballet-like slippers I was wearing.

"Damn it, Essie!" I yelled, leaning down to inspect the mess she'd made by accidentally swiping my water off the table. The drama drew unwanted eyes and made me the center of attention under the voyeuristic gaze of the other patrons in the restaurant.

"Mommy, I want it!" she crooned, standing in the booth and attempting to crawl right on top of the table to reach for my phone, which was now resting well beyond her reach.

Grabbing her by the waist, I snatched her back and hoped to nip her bratty behavior in the bud. Unfortunately, I felt my frustration creep up a notch when this little girl decided to test my patience and try to clown me by falling out in the booth.

"Auuuugggghhhh!" she moaned, fighting back at me in her flurried attempt to get to the phone.

"Sit down, Essence! And I mean now!" I spoke to her in a forceful tone, waving my arm in the hopes of summoning the waiter to come clean up the shards of glass and water.

"Just let her have it," Promise's voice added to the mayhem.

"Essence, no!" I shook my finger her way, attempting to settle her down.

"I want it!!" was her rebuttal.

Funny how much I used to want her to talk, and now that she did, she had no problem telling me what was on her little mind.

"Just give her the phone, baby. It'll settle her down," Promise persisted.

Cutting my eyes over at my mother, I frowned and shook my head to keep from lighting into her and burning off some of the frustration Essence's behavior had me feeling. If Promise knew what was good for her, she'd keep her suggestions on her side of the table.

"I'm just saying, baby, maybe it'll help," Promise offered, her voice now littered with a tone of consolation.

"Yea, well I told her to sit down. She's gonna learn to do what I tell her to do, and when I say do it," I answered while glaring at my ornery four-year-old who was squalling like someone was trying to kill her. Her outburst was so embarrassing and made me wish I was anywhere but at that table in what had been a quiet restaurant before Essence decided to show her ass. I just wanted to climb under the table, water soaked and all.

"Here baby, play with mine," Promise offered, sliding her own phone to bring it within Essie's reach. Her whimpers evaporated as she grabbed the phone, and I bit my bottom lip to stop myself from giving my mother the tongue-lashing that had been brewing and was now teetering right on the tip of my tongue.

"Don't worry, ma'am. I'll get this all cleaned up."

Our waiter was a tall, brown-skinned, handsome guy who looked to be around the same age as myself. He smiled before throwing a flirtatious wink my way, then took a broom and quickly swept away the shards of glass, allowing one of his co-workers to mop up the liquid. After replacing the drink Essie had spilled, the waiter took our food orders and disappeared off toward the back of the restaurant.

"Look at her. Nana knows what she wanted," Promise continued beaming with pride that her tactic had silenced Essie's tantrum.

"Next time, just let me handle it. I don't need you challenging me in front of her," I hissed, knocking that smile clear off her boastful face.

"Babies her age just need to be stimulated, Aniqa. Something's gotta have her attention at all times, or she'll throw those little fits."

"Do I look like I need you to tell me what she needs? 'Cause I don't! I'm her mother. I got this. In fact, I've had this for quite a long time now, and without your help," I snapped, opting to hold back most of what I really wanted to say.

For a moment, it was like the air was sucked out of the room; a good 40 seconds passed before she raised her hands in surrender. I knew I was being harsh, but the last few days hadn't been too kind to me and she was right in the line of fire, an unintended casualty of my frustration bubbling over.

"Doc!" Essie squealed with delight, pointing toward her favorite cartoon character with a smile so wide that my frustration was on pause for a second.

"She works that phone better than me," Promise noted once Essence flashed the phone in her direction, showing off the YouTube video she'd pulled up. She was right. Essence could work a phone like the process was innately engraved in her from birth. It was amazing to me how advanced toddlers were these days.

"I have some good news," Promise changed the subject as the waitress set a basket of cheddar biscuits in front of us. Grabbing one since that was the main reason I chose Red Lobster tonight, I diverted my attention back to my mother.

"I got a job lined up for myself," she announced. "I'll be working in the kitchen at the diner right up the street from where I'm staying."

"That's nice."

"And soon enough, I'm gonna get approved for an apartment. I got approved over at the Thompson SRO; you know, that old school they renovated?"

I nodded my head to let her know that I was familiar with the building she was referring to. It used to be an old elementary school that had been unused for years, and the city recently won some grant and remodeled it to help with the homeless problem in the city. There was a real big write-up about it in the papers since it gave a lot of disabled vets homes and got them off the street.

"It was converted into a bunch of efficiencies. Everything's finally coming together for me, Aniqa."

Promise's face bore a grin that showed just how pleased she was with her accomplishments.

"That's good. I'm proud of you."

My eyes darted back over to Essie, who was now switching from Doc McStuffins to some DJ Khaled song Linc had her listening to lately. My leg bounced as Promise's voice continued fading in and out with her explaining the details of her newfound sobriety. I looked toward the kitchen area, hoping that the waiter would return with our food sooner rather than later.

I hadn't spent a lot of time with my mother since Linc surprised me and reintroduced her into my life, so there was still a big ass elephant in the room whenever we were in each other's presence. I had a lot of questions and plenty of rage that I had been holding back as we eased into getting reacquainted with one another. I felt torn with her presence; happy to have her back around because I thought she was dead for so long, but upset that she'd been out there living life without me.

Even if Promise was strung out on God knows what poison, anything would have been better than having a little piece of me die every day I was under Shirlene's roof. Still, there was a lot that needed to be hashed out before we'd be able to move forward and really build something.

"You alright?" Promise asked, pulling me from the trance of my own thoughts. I cut my eyes to look up at her, tucking my temper back away into the little compartment I'd fashioned for it long ago.

"I'm good."

"You look mad," she commented. Sighing, I sat back and folded my arms across my chest, feeling the burn of my anger start to bubble up in my chest. Right at that moment, the waiter reappeared with a tray full of food.

Perfect timing.

"Sir, can we just go ahead and have that packed up to-go? I need to get out of here," I told him, finally succumbing the wave of overwhelming irritation that I felt like I could no longer fight.

"Sure," he nodded, eyeing me suspiciously while allowing his gaze to linger a little too long for my liking.

"Go 'head, pack it up for us," I told him, shooing him along.

I was probably a little more rude than I needed to be, but I realized that a part of me was still programmed to operate the way Je'Marcus had conditioned me to. Had this same situation gone down in his presence, he would've played it cool at the table, only to beat me mercilessly the minute we made it out to the car. Just the split-second thought of the deceased father of my daughter gave me an unsettling chill, but I shook it off and quickly gathered up my things to get out of the restaurant ASAP. I needed some fresh air!

By the time the three of us made it out to my car and I had Essence buckled in, the tension between Promise and I had grown considerably. The ride back to my home, which was less than five miles away, felt like a cross- country trip. After getting back to my place, I fought with Essie until she finally decided to behave and lay down for a nap, then I checked my phone to see that neither Beautiful nor Linc had called or texted me. The last thing I needed was to be left alone with my emotions, but that's exactly what my bestie and my man were doing.

For so long, I painted a mental picture of what it would take for me to be happy in life; that picture included real love with someone that loved me with his heart and not his hands, getting into college and working toward my dream of being a pharmacist, and most importantly, having my mother back in my life. I had every single item on my wish list, but this wasn't at all how I expected to feel.

I felt like Linc didn't understand me, like my best friend

didn't appreciate me, and like my mother was living in some self-righteous world where she felt like she did me a favor by coming back into my life. With everything that was swimming through my head and heart in that moment, I snapped and released an enormous helping of wrath on the only available target.

"You know, I think it's so funny how you've never truly raised a kid of your own, yet you're sitting here like you have all the right answers when it comes to my child, like I don't know what I'm doing," I unleashed on Promise the second I laid eyes on her. She had been resting on the couch flipping through one of the many magazines I had spread out on the glass sofa table.

My mother looked up at me with a surprised expression dotting her face. I knew I'd caught her off guard coming at her like that, but it was bound to come out eventually; being at odds with both Linc and Beautiful at the same time just happened to be the trigger. Seeing her face made it hard for me to forget all the shit I'd gone through as a result of her abandonment.

"Aniqa, I know I didn't do the best job raising you, but—"

"Raising me? You really call what you did raising me?" I cut her off, my voice wavering under the pregnant weight and rawness of my hurt.

At this point, my body had slipped into what felt like a series of mini-convulsions, just uncontrollable shaking that I couldn't get a grip on, and I fought to hold back the tears that were just dying to skate their way down my cheeks. I didn't want to cry. It would distract me from fully emptying the burden I'd been carrying in my heart for so long.

"If I could take it back, I would," she whispered, her voice drifting off into silence.

"Yea, but you can't take it back! Some shit you just can't take back, Promise!"

She dropped her head at the boom of my voice, and since the attack I was unleashing on her felt cleansing and uplifting, I let it all out.

"You can't take back all the shit I see in my head, all the things I wish I could forget, just everything I had to go through because you decided to leave. You didn't fuckin' love me! You couldn't have loved me with all the shit you put me through. You have no idea what kinda shit I had to deal with because of you! You know what it's like riding the school bus and having people clown me because they got pictures of you sucking some guy's dick? He was my damn classmate! You know how humiliating that was?"

The saltiness of my tears slipped onto my tongue, and I could see her bottom lip quivering.

"I went through hell because you decided you had better shit to do than be a mom to your fuckin' daughter! I was abused, I was disrespected, and all you ever did was leave! So, if you think you just showing up here, thinking your half ass accomplishments mean a damn thing to me, they don't!"

My voice shook with every word that fell from my lips as my heart galloped away in my chest; it was working feverishly to finally seep some of the long-buried agony that took up residence in my soul so many years ago. I never wanted to touch the pain, but the shit was starting to touch me– whether I wanted it to or not.

"I deserve this, I know I do."

Promise lifted her face to reveal her own sorrow. Her eyes were cloudy with emotion, and I could see that her guilt had been riding her back for years.

"I never wanted to bring you down, Aniqa," she began as her own tears started their descent toward her chest. "I thought about you every day, but I knew you were better off without me. I knew I needed to fight my problems without dragging you along. I was gonna leave you to your life, just stay completely out of the picture because I felt like you would do better if I wasn't around, but then Linc found me."

The room fell silent except for the labored respirations we both filled the air with.

"It wasn't until I got to rehab that I realized how much I needed you, how much I still need you now. As sad and pathetic as that may sound, I need you. I need you because I can't fight this thing on my own with no real purpose to stay sober. I need you because I need you to need me..."

She poured her heart out with her sobs bordering on hysteria.

"I'm s-so s-sorryyy," Promise wailed, rocking back and forth as she cradled herself.

Dropping my troubled body down onto the sofa next to her, I took deliberate breaths to calm myself, then sat in silence until she'd calmed down. I knew she was sorry. I could see it in the way her body seemed as though it wanted to fold in on itself, and though I had so much healing of my own to do, I knew my mother could only take so much. I knew she was right: she needed me, and I needed her just as much.

Letting my head fall onto the back cushions of the couch, I closed my eyes and took a deep breath...then another.

"Aniqa, I hate what I did to you, what I did to us. I hate how much you had to go through. I hate that you had to suffer. God knows I do, and I can't imagine what you had to deal with considering where you were staying. So many days, I regret ever even coming to Virginia in the first place," she vented after finally getting her bearings.

Looking over at Promise, a woman whose safety I prayed for on countless nights, I nodded in acceptance of her apology. She lifted her head to meet my gaze; unable to piece together the words that were necessary in that moment, she used her eyes to convey her message of sorrow.

As I looked into the loving eyes I'd wished for through the years, I noted that my mother was still such a beautiful woman. Despite the rough life she'd lived, the years of drug addiction and living the kind of street life necessary to support her habit, I could see that she still had a mountain of life left inside of her. She had overcome so much and still had so much to give the world. Though I didn't want to admit it, I saw pieces of myself in her.

Sighing, I wrapped her hand into my own, sending an invitation for a momentary truce while hinting at the compassion that I still had left in my heart, despite the dark roads life had taken me down.

"I have a question to ask you, and I want you to be straight up with me about this," I spoke in deliberate words, adamant that she understood the importance of my next question. Wiping the last of her tears, she dropped her gaze to the floor, took another moment to pull herself together, then brought her head back up to give me an unwavering eye contact.

"Anything," she nodded, the corners of her mouth slightly turning up into a welcoming smile.

"Where's my father?" I asked the question that had been brooding in my heart for as long as I could remember. Her hand went stiff in mine as soon as her brain registered the content and magnitude of my question, and her eyes that had been warmly examining me only seconds earlier were suddenly stone and terrified, almost as if she'd seen a ghost.

Chapter Seven

Beautiful

"Beautiful, can you calm the fuck down and let me explain?"

"It funny than a muthafucka how niggas are more than willing to explain some shit AFTER the fact."

I was so upset with this fool that I wanted to slap the shit out of him with a piece of the concrete slab I was sitting on at the moment. This nigga knew how I was, how I did business, and how I would chin-check a liar. I didn't fuck with alternative facts, and I didn't play games. Given that Tyleek had been knowing, loving, and dicking me down for years, this nigga knew better than anyone that I had no tolerance for half-truths, yet that's exactly what he'd been feeding me for the entire duration of our relationship.

"You always wildin' out over some shit that can't be changed instead of focusing on what the fuck is going on now. Damn, if you calm the fuck down then I can put you up *on game so you won't look stupid than a muhfucka—"*

WOOSH!

I was trying my best not to put my hands on him, but he hit a nerve and I had to push him out of my personal space to keep from knocking his lying ass out. I knew I needed to remove myself from his presence, but I couldn't seem to pull my feet in sync with my brain.

"Nigga, you got me fucked up! How the fuck are you going to put me up on some shit you never should've dragged me into in the first place!"

Leek was quiet at this point, which was funny because he seemed to have a whole lot to say during the phone conversation I walked in on that morning.

"Beautiful, you can either shut the fuck up and get this shit straight from the horse's mouth, or you can keep acting like one of these ghetto ass birds and just hear the shit when everyone else does. Put your hands on me one more time, though, and I swear you gon' feel me."

Now, I knew Leek would never put his hands on me, but I also know that if he was threatening to, I'd pushed him to 'that' point. As angry as I was with him, I didn't want to play around with seeing how far I could push him right now. Any other time, though? Yeah, it would have been a contact game of 'Let's Make a Deal.'

BEEP! BEEP! BEEP!

I was on my third round of snoozing my alarm, and I would have gone for a fourth had my bladder not been screaming for me to get my ass up or risk lying in a warm puddle. That dream was reason enough for me to want to put some space between myself and my bed as well. That last face-to-face conversation between Leek and myself used to play out in my head so frequently that I had to make a conscious effort to *not* think about it. He'd wiggled his way back into my thoughts with all the shit Niq and my mom were giving me about letting him see TJ. I loved my little man to death, but I'd be lying if I said I didn't wonder what it would be like to have made TJ with a man that was actually present to help me raise him.

Shaking away the irritating drone of that dream and the unwelcome thoughts of Leek, I dragged my bones out of bed and took a second to get my bearings together after I sat up.

"The fuck?" I frowned as I capped off a deep yawn.

I smelled and even thought I tasted bacon and French toast in the air, but TJ wasn't a chef last time I checked, so I put my bladder on pause, pulled on my robe, and speed-walked out of my room and up the hall toward my kitchen to see what the fuck was going on.

"Good morning, sunshine! I knew this bacon would get them hips out of bed. Go on and have a seat. I'm just about done with the eggs, so let me fix a plate for you."

My mother never ceased to amaze me, and I should have known she'd make her way over here and extend an olive branch to make amends for our disagreement. Shoot, I was too stubborn to be the first one to try to clear the air; plus, she knew the quickest way to snatch me up out of my feelings was through my stomach.

"Morning, Mama. Let me clean up and get TJ up first. I didn't realize I'd slept this late."

Ignoring my alarm was my norm, but I was dog tired last night and just couldn't deal this morning. I probably would've appreciated the few extra minutes of sleep had Leek not bullied his way into my subconscious. To make matters worse, TJ was now going to miss morning Show & Tell in his class, which was his favorite part of the day.

"No need, I already dropped him off. I got this."

Mama winked at me before returning her attention to the skillet of eggs she was preparing.

I appreciated everything my mom did for me and TJ, and honestly, I don't know if I would have been able to adjust to being a single parent if I didn't have her in my corner. Deep down, I knew she was speaking the truth the other day; I just didn't want to hear it, but there was no way in hell I'd admit it to her. I was definitely in my feelings when I snapped at her, and I knew I owed her an apology because the last thing she needed to do was to be stressing about me and my baby daddy issues.

"Mama, I'm sorry about the other day..."

"You may apologize, yes, but I didn't give birth to a sorry daughter," she shot back, feigning annoyance at my choice of words.

"How 'bout this: let me make it up to you because you know you could use a massage or something. On second thought, how about a pedicure because your feet look like some ashy beef jerky, Mama," I teased, motioning toward the heels of her feet that were exposed in the sandals she wore.

"Oh no you didn't try it, girl! I'll take you up on your offer, though, because I don't turn down beauty treatments. And since you woke up slick at the mouth, you can throw a manicure in. Now, how 'bout you go do something with the bird nest on top of your head because these eggs in this carton thought you were bringing them a new home for a second!"

"The lies you tell!"

I fell out laughing on my way to the bathroom to handle my morning hygiene and the wild hair that truly did resemble a bird's nest at the moment. My head looked like my bonnet ran off with the plug twice and never looked back.

I loved having moments like this with my mom, and seeing her standing there looking every bit the picture of perfect health with a huge smile on her face, I knew I made the right decision not leaving to enter the military. It was still something that I wanted to do, but I knew the military would always be there. I needed to soak up every second I could with my mom until we were completely sure that she was in the clear and in full remission.

"Now, about the other day, because you know I don't believe in ignoring disagreements..."

Mama scooped equal portions of her famous, fluffy scrambled eggs onto our plates, then returned the skillet to a now-cooling stovetop. I didn't realize the aroma of the meal she was preparing had my stomach growling until it spoke up so loud that it sounded like an additional party to our conversation.

"It's all good, Mama. I heard everything you said, and I appreciate that you care so much about my baby."

"What? No smart aleck comeback? Come here."

She extended her head in my direction and leaned over the counter to touch my forehead.

"You can't be my child..."

"I'm serious, Mama. You made some good points, and I promise to think about it all to make sure that I do what's best for TJ. Now, what made you come over so early?"

Mama was back at work, and though she worked from home, it was rare for her to leave the house before lunchtime. She usually spent the morning sorting through emails and addressing student inquiries.

"Because I know my child, and if you go more than two days without stopping by the house, it means you're still being too prideful to bring your tail around and show your face, which means you're still probably upset, which means you're not sleeping. I made you, girl, so I know you."

That she did, and I loved that about her.

"I never want you to feel like I'm getting in your business, Beautiful. I just know how hard it can be when you're doing the parenting thing alone. I've been in your shoes, honey, so I know it gets tough. I raised you all on my own, and even though I don't regret a single second of it, I don't want you to make the same mistakes I did, baby."

Now that I was seated at my dining room table, Mama

got settled in her seat, then reached across the table for my hand so we could bless the food. The minute we said *Amen*, she picked her train of thought right back up.

"TJ is one of God's most precious creations, and I know that boy's going to grow up to do some big things. There's too many babies out here missing out on hugs and kisses from their village, so I'm going to do everything in my power to make sure that TJ grows up with all the love he can get. Little boys need their daddies if they're going to grow into strong men, baby."

I nodded my head, making brief eye contact with her to let her know she had my attention, but giving the greater portion of my focus to the plate of delectable food that was set before me. I was so irritated last night that I skipped dinner, so I was ravenous this morning.

"Still working on eating like a lady, I see," she teased as she watched me put away the plate of food like it would be my last meal.

"And will do it again with plate number two. You know I'm not one of those salad-eating chicks." I winked, stepping away to shovel another serving of French toast onto my plate.

"So, I was thinking... if the issue is that you just don't want to have to see Tyleek yourself, then I'd be happy to be the one to take TJ up there for you. You know, like a neutral party. I may not care for his bad decisions, but Tyleek is still my grandson's father, and I will always respect his role in TJ's life."

I took a minute to think about my moms' offer, and to savor the way this French toast was melting on my tongue like a helpless ice cube. It really was a good idea, and yes, one of the main reasons I didn't want my son going up to the prison to visit his father was because I, personally, didn't want to have to lay eyes on his ass.

Tyleek knew exactly how to mind fuck me, and one of the advantages of having limited phone calls was that he never got a chance to really get in his zone and try to work his magic. Mama was proposing a win-win solution, but knowing the father of my son, he'd find some other way to try to coax me up there so he could lay eyes on me himself.

I hadn't been face to face with him since the day he got arrested; refusing to attend any of his hearings, I wanted to make it crystal clear that I wasn't one of those dumb ass ride or die chicks that would sing a man's praises when he was living foul. A chick would swear up and down that the system had done her man wrong, knowing damn well that the nigga had killed a family of four, a dog, a guinea pig, and a goldfish. Yes, I still loved Tyleek, but I refused to be *that chick* that kept her life on pause in the hopes of the nigga being released on some sort of technicality.

"Uh huh, I see you over there thinking about it. I don't know why you insist on deluding yourself that you're a thug when you know damn well you're as soft as a gummy bear on the inside."

I opened my mouth to reply, but a knock at the door snatched both of our heads away from our meal and conversation.

"You expecting someone, baby?"

"Nope, so whoever it is better be dying because anyone that has my address knows I don't play that pop-up mess. I'm antisocial for a reason."

I left my mother at the table and headed toward the door, squinting to look through the peephole when I got there.

"Oh hell no, what the fuck does this bitch want?" I mumbled under my breath when I saw who it was.

"Didn't you almost get your ass whooped the last time you brought your messy ass over here?" I boomed the minute I swung the door open and came face to face with Kay-Kay, my mom's sister.

"Well, hello to you too. Khadra, I really thought you raised this evil little heffa with more class than this," Aunt

Kay-Kay huffed, moving past me like she received an invitation to enter.

"Who the fu—"

"What do you want, Kay?" Mama interrupted.

My mother was probably the only other person that disliked my aunt as much as I did, though she wasn't as vocal about it. She despised my aunt's manipulative ways and resolved that she'd get her karma in the end.

"Oh, so it's a family affair with the rudeness this morning, I see. Now, where is Tiara, because I know you probably did something to her!" my aunt snapped.

Shit, any other time, she probably would've been right by assuming that I'd laid hands on Tiara, but I honestly hadn't seen or heard from the bitch since she showed up at my house talking all that shit about Savage having another chick off in the cut.

"Don't nobody give a fuck about that hoe. You better ask ya man where she is because you two are cut from the same cloth; always jumping at the chance to be all up in a nigga's face, knowing he has a woman."

I tried not to curse as much as I usually did when my mother was around, but fuck it. My mom knew I couldn't stand Kay-Kay's scandalous ass.

"Kay, nobody has seen Tiara, and why would you think Beautiful would know where she is? It's not like they hang out."

"Oh, this heffa knows something–"

"Bitch, you got me fucked up standing in my house talking shit!"

That was it. I lunged in her direction, but she did right by jumping back and allowing my mother to slide between the two of us.

"Tiara told me about you acting all crazy and putting your hands on her because you didn't wanna hear the truth about the no-good dude you call yourself talking to now! You just can't seem to keep a man, can you, girl?"

"You know what? We're not even about to do this, Kay. Like I said, nobody has seen your child, so you can go on and remove yourself from our presence because next time, I'm gonna let Beautiful go on and dish out that beating she's been itching to give you for some years now."

"Ain't nobody stutting you or this wild ass girl!" my aunt barked. "Let me find out you know where Tiara is and I'll be back. Ain't nobody scared of you, chile."

"I don't need you to be scared– I just need your ass to be aware!"

"Bye, Kay."

My mom pushed Kay-Kay back toward and out of the front door. I heard my aunt mumble something before my mother closed the door and spun around to face me. I could tell from the look on her face that we were thinking the same thing.

"And if someone *did* do something to her, she probably deserved it," I added, giving voice to the train of thought that hung in the air between me and my mother.

"Don't say that, Beautiful. She's still family."

"That's your family. I don't claim strays," I corrected, moving back into the dining room to clear the table and set our plates in the sink.

It had been weeks since my run-in with Tiara, and if she had been missing since she sped away from my apartment that day, it couldn't have been on good cause. There's no telling who or what she might have run up on that had handled her ass, but Tiara was so messy and stayed in so much shit that nothing would surprise me. She was on my list for trying to stir up shit between me and Savage. Add to that the fact that she kept trying to throw her pussy at Linc knowing he had a girl now, and Tiara was definitely due for some karma or revenge— whichever caught up with her ass first.

Chapter Eight

Savage

O n some real shit, I think she's tellin' the truth, bruh. She's just as vested in the business as you and your pops, so shit, if y'all hot then she hot."

Linc was still in Colorado trying to get a handle on things out there, and what he hoped would be a quick turn and burn had turned into an extended trip. There was a time when we were always at least five steps ahead of the law, but as of late, it felt like them boys had taken a crash course in how to launch a sneak attack. They kept coming at us through little cracks in the foundation that we didn't even know were there, but not for long. The stuff that went down at Mique's place was just confirmation that we needed to close ranks, handle any and every snake in our midst, and get our shit together.

Linc felt like there was some truth in whatever details Mique had given him, but unfortunately, any trust that he had for Mique was dead the minute he found out she was fuckin' Kappo. Yea, Mique was foul for that shit and had this sneakiness about her that irritated the fuck out of Linc, but even he knew that she lived for Big Linc's approval at the end of the day. Just off the strength of always wanting to keep her pops happy, I didn't think she would ever do anything to intentionally jeopardize the business.

"Nigga, I don't even care about all that. Her ass is caught up in some shit, so she's gonna say whatever she think a nigga needs to hear to get off her back, but I peep game and I got something for her. As far as I'm concerned, she's in the same category with the rest of these niggas that have been on some foul shit."

"All I'm sayin' is that everybody makes mistakes, and she's still fam at the end of the day. You know good and well that you ain't gon' be right with ya moms or ya pops if you don't find a way to fix shit with Mique," I tried to explain to my boy.

Linc and his family were the closest thing I had to family myself, and the last thing he needed was to be beefin' with his parents over some shit he refused to squash with his sister.

"Shit, Mique's mistake just happened to be fallin' on that nigga Kappo's dick." I chuckled, but to be honest, the whole situation with the two of them had me confused.

Kappo was damn near old enough to be her pops, and the nigga had a whole family and was still puttin' babies up in his wife, so why would Mique risk feeling her pops' wrath over some shit that she knew was only temporary?

"Bruh, never let that shit come out your mouth again. I'm not tryin' to hear my sister's name in the same sentence with that nigga's dick– ever again!" Linc snapped, and his irritation only made me crack up even more.

"The fuck is so funny? I'm not playin', nigga. Shit, it's cold as fuck out here and while you're back there catchin' that fade from Beautiful's crazy ass, I'm out here trying to make sure my nuts don't freeze up and get stuck to my leg and shit!"

"Yoooooo, you wild as a muthafucka, nigga!"

I lost it and gave in to the belly full of laughter that I'd been holding back. My boy sounded hella aggravated, but that shit was comical to me.

"Well, I got some shit that's gonna kill that dumb ass laugh you caught up in today. My nigga, that bitch Tiara is Kappo's seed."

"Come again, bruh? Because I know you ain't just spit the shit I think I heard."

This was some ill shit!

"And apparently, Mique knew the shit, nigga."

"Yo, what the fuck?" I frowned; this was like some Twilight Zone shit.

"Same question I have, but we'll dead all this shit in a minute. Muthafuckas are just ice-skating around and through our shit like they don't know what time it is..."

"No doubt. So, what's the move? All you gotta do is say the word, my nigga, you already know that."

Aside from the fact that I wanted to lay hands on her for blowin' my spot up to Beautiful, I couldn't stand that bitch Tiara. She was scandalous as fuck, and I told my nigga Linc that shit from day one. All ass ain't good ass, and she was a prime example of that. Her ass was too fuckin' eager to get all up in Linc's personal shit, like shit related to the business, and that always felt suspect as hell to me. Now, I had to wonder if my boy had been talking in his sleep or got caught up in some pillow talk where he said more to her than he intended to. No way in hell was it a coincidence that she just happened to wind up fuckin' the son of the nigga her pops worked for.

"Don't move on it yet. Let me check a few more things out because this needs to be a one and done type move."

"Bet. What's good with Niq? You need me to fall through and make sure her and lil' mama are good?"

"Man, I'm good on her right now."

"Nigga, what the fuck did you do now? Shorty stay beefin' with you about something."

I could tell just by his response that Linc and Niq were into it again, and most likely, it was some simple shit. My boy was in love with that girl, so I knew he wouldn't do anything too serious to fuck up what they had. I don't even think he realized just how much he was already thinking and moving like they had exchanged vows and shit, but I was happy for my boy. This nigga had been curving chicks for the longest whenever he felt that commitment shit creeping up, so I was happy to see him finally give in and let a chick get close to him. Hopefully, I could be doing the same shit soon, but Beautiful needed to find some act right and stop tryin' to take a nigga's head off all the damn time.

"Bruh, you know you can lay ya cards face-up with me. What's goin' on with y'all now?"

"Like I said, I'm good on her right now, but what else did you dig up about this fuckin' warrant?"

I knew to leave shit alone once he changed the subject. Whatever was going on with them, either it wasn't serious enough to speak on, or it was some shit he needed a minute to think on. I figured if it was something serious, I'd hear about it from Bee anyway— once she was through being mad at a nigga.

"Check game, though. They been watchin' Mique's ass for a minute now— as in *since ya pops got arrested*. Home and business, but ain't no way the law would have been able to put all that shit together on their own, so it's most def some inside shit, and you know who my money is on."

Linc got quiet for a second while he processed what I said.

"No doubt. Aight, I'mma handle that and then I'mma get the fuck up out of lil' Antarctica. Nigga, I sneezed today and my tongue got stuck to my damn lip because it was so cold. Shit's crazy, and I don't see how the fuck Mique does this shit," Linc grumbled, which only stirred my laughter up again.

"Nigga, getcho goofy ass off my fuckin' phone!"

Linc hung up in my ear, but it was cool because I needed to get across town and meet up with his pops anyway. If shit went right, I'd have some good news to hit Linc with later on.

No matter how crazy shit was right now, I loved it, loved feeling that twinge of anxiety in my stomach from not knowing what new shit we would have to fix to keep the business on course. I needed this business-type shit to keep my mind occupied because my head was still heavy with the load Emani had laid on me the other night. On the other end of things, I had Beautiful ready to cut a nigga's nuts off when I hadn't even really done shit yet. Normally, yes, I'd give a bitch 99 reasons to wild out, but I could honestly say that I had been so preoccupied with Beautiful and business that I didn't even have time to entertain these other bitches, not even if I wanted to.

I knew Beautiful and I would eventually need to have a raw and uncut conversation about Emani, especially since it was lookin' more and more like I might have to step in and take care of lil' man for Mani. Shit was still scary because a big part of me was wondering how the fuck I was gonna pull it off. I didn't know shit about kids other than pacifying them with candy or toys when they started acting up– oh, and my phone because Bee's lil' man was good for finessing my phone up out my pocket so he could play games.

Trying to forget all thoughts of Emani, her son, Beautiful, and all the other random shit that was floating through my head, I shifted my ride into drive, eased onto the highway, and headed across town to see what Big Linc had cookin' today. Since he rarely hit me up directly, I figured it had to be some serious shit that couldn't wait until Linc got back in town.

"All this fucking money I pay you clowns, all this big shit

you talk about this being like taking candy from a baby, and nobody has a fucking answer for this shit!"

Big Linc had one of those Barry White voices, so his timbre easily bounced off the walls, giving the building a slight tremble as it floated out to my ears before I even made it inside the building good. It took a lot to get him worked up, so if he was on ten like this? Yeah, there had to be some serious shit going down.

I treaded lightly and crept through the back entrance, not because I was worried about him aiming his venom in my direction, but more so because I wanted to see how this would all play out. He had a strict rule that he'd been operating by since we first met: if he had to raise his voice, someone would be leaving in a body bag.

"Explain!" Big Linc roared, directing his attention at one dude in particular.

"I-I just stepped outside f-for a second to p-piss. I held it as long as I could, and when I got back inside, the nigga was g-gone," dude stumbled over his words, offering a piss poor explanation— literally!

POW!

"Who was supposed to be on guard duty with that clown?"

Big Linc was on ten! Not even a half second after sending a hot round into Stuttering Stanley's dome, he stepped right over his body and picked up where he left off in his interrogation. I didn't know who was gone, but I hoped like hell it wasn't who I thought it was.

POW!

"Ahhhhhh shit!"

That time, Big Linc lit up the leg of the dude standing closest to him.

"I-I think it was Dame. His lil' girl was sick, though, so—"

"So, this fool said fuck work because his kid got a runny nose and shit...bet. You." Big Linc pointed at the same dude that had just spoken up. "Let that fool know his services are no longer needed, and tell him to hug his kid real tight because it's gonna be the last time he sees her. And you." He pivoted on his right foot and turned to face the other end of the line-up he had the dudes arranged in. "Get this shit cleaned up and make that fool disappear." He motioned toward Stuttering Stanley's body.

"Yo, what the fuck happened?" I probed, shaking my head as I walked past the same dudes he'd just dismissed. They all looked sick, like they were afraid to suck in too much air for fear that it would be their last breath.

"Somehow, that bitch got in here and helped the motherfucker escape!"

"What bitch?"

"The same bitch I told you and my hard-headed son I needed handled. This is the type of shit that happens when you youngsters try to outthink me, when you think you know how to play this game better than me. Now, this fool Kappo is free as a fucking bird, and there's no telling what other shit he had in the works!"

Speak of the fuckin' devil. I had to ride with Big Linc on this one: we should've bodied Tiara's sneaky ass a long time ago.

"Shit! Pops, man I gotta kick some shit down to you, and I know you ain't gon' wanna hear the shit, but it's go-time and we need to make a move ASAP."

"I love you like a son, boy, but if you have more bad news for me, I just might break my foot off in your ass today since my son isn't here to take it."

"All due respect, but that's a risk I'm gon' have to take." I paused for a second and took a deep breath because just having to utter those next words had me tight. "Tiara and Kappo are related. She's his daughter."

I wasn't afraid of Big Linc, but I took a few steps back for good measure, just because I didn't want to have to explain to Linc that I mistakenly laid his pops down while defending myself. Surprisingly, Big Linc didn't respond. He just folded his arms across his chest, rocked back and forth on his heels for a good 45 seconds, then looked up at the ceiling while gnawing away at his bottom lip.

Even though I could clearly see him standing right there before me, it was like he mentally checked out and made a run to dig up some thoughts he'd buried away in a virtual storage unit. I'd seen Linc do the same thing before when he had some heavy shit on his mind, so now I saw where he got it from.

Seeing the life come back into his face, I could see Linc's pops check back in right before he finally parted his lips to offer a response.

"Follow me," was all he said, and I fell in step without hesitation.

I loved my boy to death, but he had too much of a heart at times, and it sometimes felt like he tried to keep me on a leash when it came to ending lives. All I wanted to do was make sure we could sleep better at night, but Linc was always in thought about some shit; a real analytical planner.

However, Linc wasn't here right now, and seeing the fire dancing behind Big Linc's eyes, I just knew that there was a good chance I was gonna get to catch a body or two before the day was out. As weird as it sounds, the only thing that made my dick harder than seeing that light fade right before I snatched a nigga's last breath was feeling Beautiful's hospitable walls snatch my dick up like *she* was trying to snatch *my* damn soul.

"Close that," Big Linc ordered, motioning toward the door to his office just as I stepped one foot through the doorway. Still moving, he breezed around his desk, snatched his phone up, and dialed up whomever was programmed into #3 on his speed dial setting.

"Where are you...okay, get to your computer ASAP. Let me know when you're there," he ordered before ending the call and shifting his posture to face me. "You know what this all means, right?"

Feeling the magnitude of his words, I simply nodded and willed my dick to stay on chill as I felt a surge of adrenaline shoot out from its starting block. My skin came alive with a prickly feeling that I had come to savor and even crave at times: the calm before a fresh kill.

Chapter Nine

Linc

"Okay, well if you're not upset, then why does it feel like you're off in another country instead of just a few states away?"

"Whatchu mean?"

"Linc, this is the first time I'm hearing your voice in how many days? And when you decide to actually respond to my texts, you hit me with cold, one-word responses. You don't see anything wrong with that?"

"Niq, I've just been busy handling business out here, that's all. There's a lot going on, and I'm just tryin' to stay focused on wrapping things up so I can get back home."

"And when has business ever stopped you from returning my calls? I'm not about to do this passive-aggressive shit with you, Linc. If you're mad, then just say you're mad so we can get past it."

Aniqa was heated, and she was so fuckin' cute when she

called herself checking me that it made my dick jump as I realized how long it had been since I felt the inside of her wetness.

"Nah, see you're the one with the games. I'm not even tryin' to get into all that right now, though. I said we good, so we good. Just leave it at that."

Truth moment. Yes, a nigga was feelin' some type of way about Niq's stubborn ass and how she didn't see a need to compromise on the shit that was important to me, but it wasn't some shit I was gonna argue with her about, especially since we'd been down this road too many times before and she knew how important family was to me. We had our issues and damn sure weren't perfect, but family was important to me. My parents had been together for 28 years, and that was some rare shit nowadays. I still didn't know exactly how they made shit work given how different they were, but I did know that I wanted the kind of bond that my parents had. I felt like Niq was the one I was supposed to build that bond with, but sometimes I felt like trying to love her was more work than anything else.

I empathized with the fact that Niq never really had a real family, and I knew the concept of holding family down with unconditional love wasn't something she ever really experienced, but shit, I needed her to let the past go so we could get this happily ever after that her lil' ass wrote about in her journal. Of course, I'd never invade her privacy and trespass on her innermost thoughts, but I did sneak a peek over her shoulder a few times while we were chillaxin' on the couch, and I saw how almost every page had a bunch of hearts and shit doodled in the corners; you know, the kinda shit females do when they're in love.

"I can't deal with all this, Linc!"

See, this was the shit that tripped me out about females, and I thought Niq was exempt because she seemed like she knew how to keep her emotions in check in the beginning, but it never failed. Females were just some emotionally unstable creatures, and it always felt like a crap shoot dealing with their asses. Shit could be clutch and a nigga could be having the best day of his life, then bam! The wind blows the wrong kinda pollen their way and a chick is in tears behind the shit. Then bam! She's cursing and ready to fight mother nature because the car she spent a good five minutes driving through the car wash is covered in a thin, yellow sheet of that same pollen. Shit was crazy! *So, here we go with the dramatics!*

"It's just too much! You're mad for no reason, and you won't even consider my side of things! Beautiful is mad when all I tried to do was be a good friend! Promise thinks she can just blow in like mother of the year and try to tell me how to raise my baby! Essie is about to make me slap the taste out of her mouth— I just can't do this shit, Linc!"

See what I mean? Niq was acting like it was the end of the world when, just based on what she ran down, she was most likely the reason for her own frustration. Females always took shit personal and didn't know how to let shit ride. You and your homegirl have words and run up on a difference of opinions? Table that shit and take a break, then come back with a fresh head. Nine times out of ten, you wouldn't even remember why you started beefin' in the first place and could just move past it. I wouldn't dare say that to Niq right now, though, because that would really set her ass off.

"Okay ma, calm down. I'm not mad, Niq. You don't wanna do dinner with my fam again, that's fine. I can accept that and we'll talk about it more when I get home. I still love your lil' ass, and that ain't gon' change. And you know good and well you and Bee need each other too much to stay mad for too long. Y'all love each other like sisters, and sisters fight, but sisters always make up. Now, with Promise, you gotta give your moms a break, ma. Look at things from her perspective. She's missed out on a lot of time with you and lil' mama, and more than anything, she just wants to keep you from making the same mistakes she did. Even when someone doesn't necessarily know how to do things the right way, they damn sure know how to do 'em the wrong way and if they really love you, they'll try to steer you clear of those wrong ways."

Aniqa got so quiet on the other end that I had to make sure she was still on the line.

"Yo, you good?"

When I heard her sniffle and mumble her reply, I knew she was still there.

"Niq, ya moms is just trying to find out how she fits into your life now that you're grown, that's all. Give her a break and have a lil' patience with her, aight?"

"I'll try, but she's not gonna be telling me how to run things in our home, Linc," Niq whined.

"No doubt, but don't discount everything she says like it has no value. Just because she made some mistakes, it doesn't mean she didn't learn from 'em, and when a person learns from their mistakes, they walk away with wisdom. Now, as far as my princess is concerned, I don't care what you say, she can do no wrong in my eyes, so that's probably your fault because she's always an angel with me," I teased.

"Whatever, boy! The only thing I've done is tell her no!"

"Shit, that's where you went wrong. Short stack can have whatever she wants."

"And that would be the reason she's running around here like a wild ass animal that has no home training. I swear I can't wait until you get back because I'm going to leave you alone for a whole weekend with *your princess*," Niq hissed. I smiled because I could picture the little wrinkle across the bridge of her nose as though she was sitting next to me.

"You say that shit like it's gon' be a challenge. I got lil' mama. She only tries you because she knows she has your ass shook. But let us have our weekend, and I don't wanna hear no whining or begging when we fall back through that bitch and don't bring you anything back."

Niq would have a fit whenever she felt left out of me and lil' mama's quality time, which is why I always laughed when she called Essence a brat, because where the hell did she think lil' mama got it from?

"All this shit you're talking, and I bet you'll be calling me a few hours in when you can't deal with her."

"Bet it up then. What I'mma get when I win?"

"Anything you want because I know for a fact that you're gonna come up short on this one."

"Remember you said anything, so I don't wanna hear that *'stop, it hurts'* shit. I gotta burn out, though, so I'll hit you back later and chop it up with short stack."

"Na uh! Wait a minute, what you mean—"

I disconnected the call before she could even protest. Pops was waiting for me to hit him once I made it back to my suite, and I could tell from the tone of his voice that he was in a mood.

I'm not gonna lie, it felt like a small weight had been lifted from my shoulders after talking to Niq. I hated that arguing shit, so instead of going back and forth with her while she talked over me and cut me off, I just fell back anytime we got into it. I knew that eventually, she would start to miss a nigga and try to squash shit.

Feeling shit was back on track with the home life, I shifted my focus and readied myself for whatever the fuck I was about to see and hear on this surveillance feed that Pops had pulled. I saw that the parking lot had finally been plowed as I turned into the parking lot of my hotel, so I snatched up a spot close to the side entrance and got my ass inside before the wind disrespected the shit out of my winter attire yet again. It didn't matter how you dressed out here; layers, thick sweaters, boots— NOTHING seemed to keep the cold away from a nigga's bones, and I could see why they made herb legal. Niggas needed something to make them forget how fuckin' cold it was!

"What the fuck took you so long?"

"You can't be serious right now!"

"Just get this...ahh, that shit's hot!"

While Pops and Savage were watching the feed from his office, I logged in on my end and was posted up against the headboard of the bed, right knee bent with my foot planted flat against the mattress. I expanded the video to play full screen so I could have a full view of the fuckery that Tiara and Kappo had managed to pull off. I don't even know how the fuck she knew where he was, but she managed to slither her snake ass right up in there and set him free.

What the fuck!

I needed to get back to VA ASAP!

"How the hell did you not see them coming?"

"Don't worry 'bout all that. Come on, we gotta get the fuck up outta here before that fool comes back!"

The camera gave a perfect view of Tiara's flurried attempt to set Kappo free, and now that I was looking at the two of them side by side on my screen, I could see the slight resemblance that spoke to her being his seed. It really was a small fuckin' world, and I instantly felt myself replaying every second I ever spent in Tiara's presence. This bitch was something else!

"Dad, I love you and all, but this is it. I want no more parts in any of this. I was cool with the part about Linc because he's a nice dude, but all this other stuff? I'm out, seriously."

"The fuck you mean you out? You out when I say you ou—shit! Watch that fuckin' thing!"

Unbothered, Tiara kept working, glancing over her shoulder every few seconds to make sure the coast was still clear.

"Seriously. It's only a matter of time before someone finds out about the stuff with the little girl, and I'm trying to be as far away from Linc's reach as possible."

"All the time you spent suckin' that nigga's dick and you ain't figure out how to control his ass? I see your mama ain't teach you shit!"

"Apparently, you aren't too bright yourself since you got caught up fucking this man's daughter, now are you!"

"Oh, I wanted the nigga to find out, and he ain't seen shit yet. I left that bitch breathing, but his wife might not be so lucky. And I got something for that arrogant son of his too.

That nigga might have thought he was punking me, but we gon' see what happily ever after feels like when his girl and kid are six feet deep!"

"That's not his fuckin' kid!"

"And you sound real stupid right about now, takin' up for a nigga that's gon' put a bullet in your head the first chance he gets once he finds out what you been up to."

I wouldn't have believed this shit if I wasn't seeing it with my own eyes. This nigga Kappo really had a death wish, and I was about to be his fuckin' genie since he felt boss enough to even think about coming after my family.

Listening to this nigga run down his ulterior motives, I realized that Savage was right and I should MAYBE think about giving my sister a break. This nigga basically used her, but she was too dickmatized to even see it coming.

"All these years, and this nigga thought I forgot about it...thought he was doing ME a fuckin' favor lacing my pockets when I got out, thought I was some fuckin' gump ass nigga that was gonna run his errands and do his dirty work. But the nigga fucked up and gave me an opening, and that's all I need. This shit is either gon' be mine, or it's gon' crumble. Ain't no in-between!"

"Okay, Nino Brown. Either way, I want no parts of it.

Now, hold still, I almost got it..."

"Good, and we need to make a move on white bread too–"

"What! Dad, I haven't even heard from Paxton since–"

"My point exactly. He might be quiet, but his old man is doing a lot of talking, so how 'bout we NOT sit around and wait for him to start running his mouth about #11 and shit!"

Number 11...as in the Fire House #11 where whomever snatched Essence dropped her off at? Shit really WAS crazy, and if Kappo was saying what I thought he was, shit just got REALLY real!

"Wait a sec... twist this arm to the left... I got it!"

We watched a few more seconds as Kappo sprang up out of the contraption he was chained to and rubbed his wrists as though he was trying to jump-start his circulation. He then reached out to snatch Tiara by the wrist and the two of them popped smoke as they headed off into the darkness and just out of the view of the camera.

Pops did something on his end, and our view changed to one of the cameras that was mounted to the exterior of the building. We got a clear view of Tiara and Kappo racing across the gravel and over to what I now recognized as Kappo's truck.

"Find your sister and be on the first fuckin' thing smoking back this way!" was all Pops said before he disconnected the video feed and hung up in my ear.

All hell was about to break loose, and one thing was for sure: Tiara's mama was about to grieve the loss of her daughter and her snake ass baby daddy!

Chapter Ten

Aniqa

"Mommy, we go see my Bee?"

After spending the greater portion of my week bogged down in homework, I was looking forward to sleeping in today, but my baby girl wanted no parts of that. I had gotten used to having Linc around to entertain Essie in the evenings so I could get some quiet study time in, but with him being gone so long, it had thrown my study plan off.

"Mommyyyyyyyyy, we gotta go noooooow!"

Aside from my bruised feelings, the hardest part about the rift between Beautiful and myself was not having her and TJ around as we usually did. Essie loved her some Beautiful, and with her asking for *her Bee* every day, it made me realize how silly it was for me and Beautiful to be at odds over such a trivial disagreement. I thought about all the times she'd been there for me when Je'Marcus was being his usual barbaric self, and how she'd never once judged me when she knew I would go right back to him.

At times, I felt so defeated that I couldn't even find the words to explain what happened or how I was feeling; it was during those times that she let me cry in her lap, never pressing me to talk, just letting me empty my soul until I felt strong enough to hold my head up again. She could have called me out plenty of times for being the foolish, weak baby mama that played doormat to a no-good man, but not once did she take that route.

When Ms. Khadra called and asked if me and Essie could swing by and have breakfast with her, it was perfect timing. I needed someone to talk to, and since she'd been more of a mother to me than anyone else, I knew she would have some great advice. It didn't hurt that she made the best French toast on the East coast either! I told Essence we were going to see Ms. Khadra right before I put her to bed last night, and I bet she barely got a wink of sleep because of her excitement.

"Okay, Ms. Thang, I'm up... Mommy's up. Did you brush your teeth already?"

Sure enough, she flashed a set of freshly brushed teeth at me. Pulling my weary body up into a seated position, I took in her appearance and saw that she had attempted to dress herself— that's just how excited she was. It looked like she had settled on a *Moana* hoodie, a pair of *Despicable Minions* leggings, a pink Ugg on one foot, and a Doc McStuffins flip flop on the other.

"Baby girl, what's up with your shoes?" I chuckled as I reached out to pull her up onto my lap. It warmed my heart to see my baby so happy and full of life. This was a side of her I'd only seen on a few occasions the entire time we were living under the same roof with Je'Marcus and his crazy ass family. It was long overdue, but I was happy to see my baby finally enjoying being the little doll that she was.

Essence took off running down the hall toward her room, and about half an hour later, we were both bathed, dressed, and ready to head out. I was just slipping my feet into my shoes when she came jogging into the living room with the little Doc McStuffins backpack Linc bought her on her back and my keys in her little hand.

"We go now, Mommy?"

"Yes, baby. I'm coming right now. Who's driving, you or me?" I winked, and she fell into the cutest fit of giggles as I hit the light switch so we could head out and make our way to Ms. Khadra's house. I swear it felt like my stomach was touching my back!

"I want Mars, Mommy!" Essence cheered from the back seat, so I flipped through my iTunes collection until I came to Bruno Mars' "That's What I Like," a song that would easily keep her occupied even after it had finished playing.

Even the simplest things that Essence said or did made me think of my mother. I wondered if she remembered my first step, first word, when I learned how to tie my own shoes, just all the memorable little milestones that occurred in a child's life. I knew what Linc said was right, and that I needed to let the past be the past since Promise really was making an effort at getting herself together, but I just couldn't seem to shake the anger I felt at her choosing to discard me and all those little milestones. A part of me just couldn't comprehend how she could so easily walk away and never look back, because I could never picture myself ever leaving my baby of my own free will. Yet, another part of me did understand because the same way she'd been a slave to her addiction, I'd been beholden to that same kind of addiction in the form of a man that never meant me any good.

I got so wrapped up in my thoughts that I almost missed the exit for Ms. Khadra's house, but after checking my rearview to make sure the lane was clear, I zipped over, slowed down, and caught the exit just in the nick of time.

"Wooooah, Mommy!" Essence giggled from the back seat like we were on a ride at the carnival Linc had taken her to just weeks prior. "Again, Mommy! We go again!"

"Maybe after we stop and see Ms. Khadra, okay babes?"

"Yay! My Bee!" she cheered just as I was turning down Ms. Khadra's street, and damn if my eyes didn't land on something that revealed the real reason Ms. Khadra was so adamant that we swung by for breakfast this morning: my best friend's car.

I couldn't even be mad at Ms. Khadra, though, because this mess between me and my bestie had gone on too long. I missed her craziness, and even if I had to let her fuss and cuss me out for a few minutes to purge it all from her system, I'd deal with it just to have my sister back.

Essence spotted Beautiful's car just as I pulled up into Ms. Khadra's driveway and started clapping her hands like she'd hit the Chuck E. Cheese lottery and was about to get ticket-wasted. It was in that moment that I realized how selfish it was for me and Beautiful to fall out over something that we could have easily talked our way through— either that, or just settled for the fact that we'd have to agree to disagree. If we weren't on good terms, that meant Essie and TJ were missing out on each other's company, and that wasn't fair to them. Since Beautiful had more than a few days to stew in her anger, I had no idea what I was walking into, but I took a small measure of comfort at knowing she wouldn't cut up too badly in her mom's house.

Checking my face one last time in the visor, I grabbed up the Goldfish plant I'd picked up for Ms. Khadra and rounded the car to free Essie from her booster car seat. Beautiful's mom was a green thumb extraordinaire, and she could make just about anything bloom with life; very similar to the way she made the people around her thrive. The minute Essie's feet hit the driveway, she took off running toward Ms. Khadra's front door, raining a flurry of little knocks on the screen door because she was still about a half an inch too short to reach the doorbell.

Even though she'd lured me here under somewhat false pretenses, I was thankful that I had someone like Khadra Mudarris in my life, even to the point where I felt a little guilty that I loved her with more enthusiasm than I did Promise. Thoughts for another day, though, because I'd need all the mental stamina I could muster to weather the storm that I knew would be Ms. Beautiful Mudarris.

"Ooooh, look at you, little Ms. Sunshine! I love those boots, girl! You betta work it!" Ms. Khadra's voice spilled out onto the front porch the minute she pulled the door open and saw Essence standing there looking runway ready for a Nick

Jr. fashion show.

Essence fell into Ms. Khadra's arms all dramatic, like she hadn't seen her in years, and they were spinning in circles by the time I made it up onto the porch.

"Good Morning, absentee daughter. Fix that face and come on up in here to get some breakfast and forgiveness."

Ms. Khadra read me and shut me up all in a single breath, and you know what I did? Kept my mouth shut and carried my ass inside the house to gorge myself on that bomb ass French toast.

"Mama, I moved the other load over to the dryer, but you're out of—"

My bestie breezed into the room unexpectedly, moving with a purpose, but stopping dead in her tracks when she saw me standing there. Tense wasn't even the word to describe the pregnant anxiety that hung in the air between the two of us. I could see Ms. Khadra out the corner of my eye, and though she busied herself in the kitchen after getting Essie seated at the table to color with TJ, I knew she was loosely taking in the exchange between the daughter she birthed and the daughter she'd adopted by heart.

Beautiful just stood there boring a hole through me with her gaze, giving a deliberate head-to-toe examination as though she were seeing me again for the first time. Just when I thought she was about to hit me with the silent treatment, she proved me wrong and showed why there would never be a dull moment in her presence.

"All that damn money Linc is papered up with, and you still leave the house with ashy ankles. Mama, you got some lotion for this lil' dusty girl?"

"Right next to the superglue I'm gonna use for your lips if you don't find something nice to say," Ms. Khadra lobbed, not even looking up from the food she was plating.

Beautiful rolled her eyes and breathed a real deep sigh, like she was searching for just the right response that would allow her to be smart aleck and PG-rated all in one.

"Okay, you look *cute* and dusty... like a powdered donut." She rolled her eyes before turning her attention to her second-favorite person in the world.

"Little miss diva, girl you better work those cute lil' boots! Lemme see 'em!"

Essence didn't give TJ or those crayons a second thought as she sprang up out of her seat and ran into Bee's arms. No matter how dysfunctional, I loved the family I inherited the day Beautiful brought me home one day after school in sixth grade— now, I was *definitely* dusty back then.

"Ohh, Aniqa, can you do me a favor since I see my child is still walking around in pajamas?"

"You bet, Ms. Khadra, what's up?"

"Run up the street and grab some orange juice because *somebody* drank the last little bit and left an empty carton in my fridge."

She cut her eyes at Beautiful to put emphasis on just who that *somebody* was. After dodging the twenty-dollar bill that Ms. Khadra tried to press into my palm, I was back out the door to make what I hoped would be a quick store run because that French toast? Man, the aroma alone had my esophagus twerking in anticipation of the blessing it knew was on the way.

The main access road that led to the store was blocked off, and I didn't want to take the back way and cut through the neighborhood because it was pothole city, so I decided to take another route that would cut through the small forest separating Ms. Khadra's neighborhood from the next one over. It was an extra mile out of the way, but it would put me right at the entrance for the store and be a smoother ride than all those damn potholes.

I realized Linc still hadn't responded to my text from earlier and decided to give him a call and check in with him real quick. He was finally flying back, and even though I still wasn't completely sold on the idea of dinner with the rude ass Mrs. Carmichael, I was just glad he was coming–

BOOM!

"What the fu–"

BOOM!

"Shit!"

On instinct, I tightened my grip on the steering wheel and tried to correct my path and ease back onto the road, but–

BOOM!

I felt excruciating pain as my head alternated between bouncing off the steering wheel, headrest, and window. I couldn't see what was going on, but I could feel the car flip I don't know how many times before I felt it slam into something. Wide-eyed with panic, I still couldn't see a damn thing, but I felt something warm running down my face right before I felt this fuzzy feeling ooze all over my body, starting at my head. I knew it was fairly warm outside, but I felt so cold and so sleepy...so, I closed my eyes and went to sleep...

Chapter Eleven

Beautiful

Shit wasn't supposed to happen like this. Hell yeah, I knew Mama had invited Niq and Little Essie over this morning; she'd given me an hour-long dose of act right and said neither of us was leaving her house until we squashed whatever conflict we were having. I missed my lil' goddaughter, and TJ had been bugging me about seeing *his E.* Even though I didn't show it, I was happy to see Niq's short ass standing in Mama's hallway, but shit, things weren't supposed to go this way— with this haggard-looking doctor giving us a rundown of Aniqa's condition and the extent of her injuries. His ass looked like he was half asleep, but for his sake, I hoped he was truly awake and alert because if he even spelled my sister's name wrong, I'd gladly help him make the transition from physician to patient.

"Ms. Haddon was unconscious upon arrival, and given the nature of her injuries, it's nothing short of a blessing that the passing motorist rode by when he did. A few more minutes and it's likely she would have bled out, so she's a very lucky young woman."

"Not lucky, blessed," Mama corrected as she shifted her purse from one shoulder to the other.

"Indeed, ma'am. Extremely blessed."

"We go see Mommy, Bee?"

Little Essie's voice was soft with a shaky hint of uncertainty as she spoke. Of course, she didn't know exactly what was going on, but kids were more perceptive than adults realized, so I'm sure her little stomach was in knots from the fact that we were in the hospital.

"In a minute, dollface." I forced a smile in an effort to give her some reassurance while nodding to my mother to take her back over to where TJ was seated. I didn't want her hearing any more about Niq's condition than necessary.

"Is she going to be okay, Doctor? I mean... will she wake up?"

There wasn't a lot of shit that scared me in life, but losing someone I loved was something I didn't even want to have to think about. I felt like we'd just made it to sure ground with Mama's condition, but just as soon as we were in the clear and she was officially in full remission, this shit happened.

"Oh, she's been in and out of consciousness since they

brought her in. According to the first responders, it looks like her vehicle flipped a few times after it left the road, leaving her pretty banged up. I'll be frank with you, ma'am. Ms. Haddon has quite a long road to recovery, but I have no doubt that she'll make a full recovery."

"Long road?"

"Yes. She sustained a severe fracture to her right jaw, and we'll need to do a closed reduction. Wiring the teeth together will essentially function like a cast, holding the jaw into place to restrict movement and expedite proper healing."

"Shit!"

"It will be painful at first, but as time progresses, Ms. Haddon will get used to the arrangement and experience more frustration than pain. The number one complaint we hear from patients is not being able write as fast as they talk." The doctor chuckled, and I appreciated his attempt to lighten the mood, but damn! Niq wouldn't be able to talk for weeks? This was about to be some interesting shit!

"Ms. Haddon has a few other minor fractures to her face, a broken pelvis, shattered kneecap, and a broken rib, but considering the severity of the accident, it's nothing short of a miracle that she didn't suffer more trauma," the doctor finished, and I finally released the breath that I didn't even realize I'd been holding hostage.

After seeing the gnarled wreckage of what used to be Linc's SUV, I knew the doctor was right. The minute we got the call, I was peeling out of the driveway and speeding down to a scene that I was almost afraid to see. When I saw how the front of Linc's truck was hugging the tree so tightly that they appeared to be two long-lost lovers, I felt sick at what might be Niq's fate. Hearing this doctor stand before me and declare that she was going to be alright, I was powerless to stop the trail of tears that told just how much relief was swirling within my chest.

The doctor extended a hand to give me a gentle pat of reassurance on the shoulder before wrapping up his update on Niq's condition.

"The nurses are getting her settled in a room now, so give or take a few hours and you all can go up and see her," he advised just as he was paged over the hospital's intercom. I heard Mama's footsteps behind me just as I swiped the last of my tears away.

"God has this thang all worked out for her, baby. For us all. She's covered, and she's His child, so we already know she's going to be just fine," Mama encouraged.

I did an about-face and saw that Mama had successfully distracted Essence with an activity book, and it looked like she and TJ were engrossed in solving a missing object page together. I thought about all the shit Niq had gone through since we first met, from not having a real home to living in a home that was more like a prison. I thought about all the times she tried to hide the bruises, the cuts, the swelling from the most recent explosion of Je'Marcus' rage. I even remembered the exact point where she pretty much gave up trying to hide the evidence of his abuse and instead, pleaded with her eyes for me to just let things be as they were. Niq had been dealt a fucked-up hand in life, no doubt about it, but she'd also overcome a lot to get where she was.

Seeing what was left of Linc's SUV was a wake-up call to me that we had to do better than to let such a trivial thing push us into such a stupid conflict, especially to the point where we weren't on speaking terms. Well, I guess I was the one that had been mostly stubborn and ignored her calls and texts because I felt like she needed to suffer a little bit more, like she needed to hurt since I was hurting. Either way, the shit was childish, and I intended to make it right. More than anything, I intended to make sure my godbaby kept right on being the happy little girl that she was. I just hoped the doctor was right and things didn't get too much worse before they got better.

Mama had just left about thirty minutes prior to take the kids to grab something to eat when a nurse came down to let me know that Niq was ready for visitors. I don't think my feet ever felt as heavy as they did during my walk to the elevator, and as I rode up to the third floor, all I could think about was how right both Mama and Niq were about TJ. If anything ever happened to me and I left this earth, I'd want my baby to have as strong a network of support as he possibly could, whether he was still a child or was an adult and on his own. No matter how much I didn't like it, that network should probably include his father, and I promised myself that as soon as I made sure my sister was good and Essence was settled, I'd take the first steps in getting TJ up to visit Tyleek.

"Oh, I'm so sorry!" a nurse rushed as we collided when the elevator doors slid open. I normally would've let her know just how sorry she really was, but instead, I just brushed the incident off and slipped back into my bout of tunnel vision, moving down the hall with a sense of urgency as my eyes hopped from one placard to the next in search of Niq's room. There was a nurse coming out just as I reached the right door.

"The sedation is just wearing off, so she's extremely groggy. I just gave her another dose of medicine to kick in before the sedation completely wears off. It will keep her calm and help relax her airway so she can breathe properly. It's important to keep her as calm and settled as possible in these first few days, so no laughing, and let's try to hold off on any topics or conversations that might make her emotional," the nurse advised, moving past me as I stepped into the room and had my first look at Niq since she left Mama's house in search of orange juice.

Niq had the natural sort of beauty that was best appreciated in the absence of tons of makeup, but her once mocha complexion was now a bloated kaleidoscope of purples and greens, courtesy of the bruises and abrasions that were starting to make their presence known. Shit, I was so glad Essence hadn't been in the car with her!

She started to stir, though she couldn't move much since they had her in traction to ease some of the pressure on her pelvis. I stifled a laugh when I saw that her means of communication was reduced to a dry erase board and a marker that was just beyond her reach. She did her best to scrawl her message in a shaky penmanship that looked like it could've been Essence or TJ's writing.

"She's fine. Mama is probably stuffing her and TJ with Chick-Fil-A right about now," I offered as she scribbled another message.

"He's on his way back and said he'd come straight here the minute his plane lands," I advised, now thankful that Savage had texted me an update on Linc's whereabouts just minutes before the nurse alerted me that I could head up to visit Niq.

Linc's sister had forgotten her ID, so they missed their first flight and were rebooked on another one that left a few hours later, and glancing at my watch, it looked like he was due to land in roughly half an hour.

Niq paused and the furrow in her brow deepened; it looked like she was in deep thought as she scrawled something else on the board.

"I tried to reach her at the number you have for her, but she still hasn't called me back."

I was still on the fence about whether or not Niq's mom was full of shit or had really gotten her shit together and cleaned herself up. Maybe it wasn't right, but I didn't have a whole lot of optimism when it came to addicts. As far as I was concerned, an addict was always one stressor away from slipping back into their old habits, and I was especially protective of Aniqa and Essence for obvious reasons. Mama loved Niq like she had given birth to her, but I knew it had to feel fucked up to be left behind by the woman that had labored to push you into the world. Promise was still suspect in my book, and I wasn't entirely convinced that this sudden reappearance in Niq's life came without ulterior motives. Yes, I was happy that my friend had her mother back; I knew how many nights Niq spent feeling like she might be somewhere dead. Still, I had every intention of keeping my eye on Promise, and only when /felt like she'd earned her spot back in Niq's life would I back off.

Niq was busy scribbling again, and I could see her eyes well up with tears at whatever was weighing on her heart.

"O-okay, calm down, girl. Can you do me a favor? Just breathe, but do it slow..." I tried my best to coach Niq to relax, even taking deep breaths of my own to emulate the action I needed her to focus on in that moment. It seemed to work, and though I still saw a lone tear sneak down her cheek, I could see her making the effort to calm herself down, almost as though she was drawing a sense of peace from the fact that I was calm.

"Yes, you will be able to walk again, girl. You are going to be just fine. That doctor gave me his word, and you already know what the fuck is gonna go down if that muthafucka lied to me, right?"

Niq's mouth attempted to spread into a smile, but feeling the taut pull of the wiring procedure, she settled for a half smile and scribbled that I was crazy on her little board.

"Says the girl that's up in here looking like yesterday's wrinkled sheets."

After helping her find the OWN channel so she could watch the season one marathon of *Greenleaf*, I fluffed the pillows behind her head to make sure she was able to stay upright as the nurse had advised. Though her gaze was set on the flat panel TV, Niq had this faraway look in her eyes that let me know she was deep off in the recesses of her brain, digging through who knows what thoughts. I figured that her current circumstances had likely stirred thoughts of the life that she was drowning in that day she bumped into Linc Carmichael in Walgreens several months prior.

If the hospital had one of those frequent visitor loyalty cards, Niq would have surely been in the running as one of the faces that they saw on the regular. Je'Marcus kept her on a frequent rotation of ER visits, where she'd lie and pass her injuries off as the result of a bicycle accident or mishap during a kickboxing match— I tell you one thing: Niq had an imagination out of this world, and the bullshit excuses she concocted were so damn convincing that I'd believe them if I didn't know the truth myself.

Either way, I knew that I now had a new mission to ensure my girl could get back to living that happily ever after she so rightly deserved with Linc. I had to keep her mind as far away from her past as possible and focused on the future she had with Linc, Essie, and shit, even Promise's questionable ass.

I pulled my eyes from Niq long enough to check the text message I'd just received and saw that Mama was back downstairs with the kids. We'd already decided that it might be best to hold off on letting the kids see Niq for a few more days; that way, some of the swelling and discoloration could fade and they'd be less likely to be afraid at what they saw.

"Niq, me and Mama are gonna switch out, so let me run downstairs and get the kids, and she'll come up here to sit with you for a while, okay? I'll try to reach Linc to see how much longer it'll be before he gets here, and I'll send Mama a message to let her know so she can pass it along to you, okay?"

I saw a brief shadow of sadness pass across her face, but she quickly shook it off and gave me what looked like it would be her signature smile as long as her mouth was wired shut. After planting a kiss on her forehead, I slipped out of her room and trekked back down the hall toward the elevator, sending up a silent prayer of thanks that I hadn't lost my sister.

Thoughts wandering aimlessly, I eyed the digital display that tracked the elevator's descent from three floors up. I was still riding those thoughts when the elevator finally dinged its arrival. The doors slipped apart a few seconds later, and I got an unexpected surprise at the sight of the lone person that already occupied the elevator car, especially since he supposedly had something urgent to tend to across town.

"Savage? What are you doing here?"

Chapter Twelve

Savage

I didn't know if the moon was in its full phase or what, but today had been a fucked-up day! First, I woke up to find that some lil' knucklehead muhfuckas tried to steal my shit out of my car. Then, Beautiful hit my phone with a text looking for Linc and said Aniqa had been in an accident or some shit.

I was already on my way to the hospital when I got Bee's text because I got a call earlier that Mani was in pretty bad shape, and her family needed to get there ASAP. Since she had no family, she'd listed me as her next of kin. I could tell from the doctor's tone that things were bad, but the shit I walked in on when I entered her room? That shit had me fucked up in the head!

The doctor that called wouldn't gimme a lot of info over the phone, and I could now see why. Mani looked like death. Her eyes were sunken, flesh was clammy, and the beautiful color that usually lined her flesh was gone. I couldn't believe what the fuck I was looking at.

"As I'm sure you know, her immune system is especially weakened and compromised as a result of the renal failure. She's contracted an infection that seems to be resistant to the antibiotics she was prescribed a few weeks ago, which has caused her kidneys to stop responding to the dialysis. Our best estimate is 72 hours, so if you know of any other loved ones, it would be best for them to get here as soon as possible."

Even after the doctor left, I could still hear that *72 hours* echoing in my head, but that shit just seemed unreal. Emani was the first chick I ever gave a fuck about; shit, the first chick I loved, and even though I had long given up hope that we could somehow find a way to make shit work, a nigga still took comfort in knowing she was just a phone call away. It felt like too many years had slipped past us, and my head was all fucked up because I couldn't see how the hell I could say goodbye to her for the last time.

"Did you bring them?" Mani spoke with a whisper that was so soft I had to strain my ears to hear.

Nodding my reply, I pulled the packet of stapled papers from my back pocket and unfolded them. Truthfully, I had signed the papers the same night she gave them to me, but I had them notarized just yesterday. I didn't consciously plan to, but something went off in my head, almost like an alarm, and it had me pulling up in front of the UPS store before I even realized where I was headed.

I stepped closer to her bed and placed the papers in her left hand, and after squinting at them to adjust her gaze, she confirmed that they were signed and notarized before forcing a weak smile up at me.

"Thank you, Sampson. This means so much to me," she mouthed.

I didn't realize my eyes were leaking until I felt the tears plop onto my hoodie, but I wasn't even trippin'. Mani was the only chick I felt like I could fully let my guard down with, so I ain't give a fuck if she saw me cry. I was hoping to get to this point with Bee someday, but since she stayed mad at a nigga more often than not, I didn't know if we'd make it.

"Save those tears... I'm okay with this. I prayed and accepted what's to come, so I'm okay. Now that I know my baby is in the best possible hands, I'm even better," Mani smiled.

My face slipped into a frown at the mention of her son, and I instantly wondered where he was when Mani collapsed and had to be rushed to the hospital. Like she'd done many times before, she read my thoughts and answered the question before it had a chance to leave my lips.

"He's with my neighbor, Ms. Pamela. You remember the

lady that used to babysit him back in the day?" I nodded. "I dropped him off earlier so I could run to the store... guess that was for the best now."

Emani's eyes misted with tears that I could see her struggling to hold back, which kicked off a fresh wave of my own.

"Dre's a smart kid, Sampson. I had a talk with him, so he knows what to expect. Just... just never let him forget me," she pleaded, voice cracking as though it took every bit of her energy to speak. "Promise me that, please?"

A nigga wasn't built for emotional shit like this, and I didn't see how the fuck nurses and doctors lived through this every day, watching people lay around and wait for death to take 'em over to the other side. The shit felt unreal to me. Mani was too young to be saying anything close to final goodbyes. Shit just wasn't right.

"Sampson... look at me." I held my breath for a few seconds to kill the fresh wave of tears that were tryin' to force their way down my face.

Very few people could get away with using my government name; very few people except Emani. Standing there looking at her for what might be the last time, my mind raced through so many memories I had of her, memories that kept a nigga goin' when I was counting the days until I'd be free again. In a lot of ways, Mani was the chick that made a nigga grow up. She knew her worth and was quick to let it be known that she wasn't to be played. She demanded respect, but with a quiet and soft-spoken power that made you lean in and listen to make sure you didn't miss anything — the complete opposite of Beautiful's loud and no-filter havin' ass.

"It's okay to let her in... but make sure you do right by her. If you can't, then don't waste her time and break her heart. No woman deserves that. You're a good dude with a good heart... let her see that." Mani's words were slow and deliberate, not as though she was unsure, but more like she was trying to ration her energy to make sure she got her intended message across.

I was locked in my thoughts for a few seconds, turning Mani's words over in my head, thinking of how letting Bee in was about to take on a whole new meaning. A few seconds later, I was jarred from my thoughts when Emani waved me over closer to her bed with a frail hand. Now standing just a few inches from where she lay, I accepted her invitation and took her hand into mine as I took a seat in the nearby chair.

"Pray with me?"

Do what? Man, I ain't know the first thing about praying, like seriously praying, but how the hell could I deny Mani's request given her present condition?

Figuring I could fake it 'til I made it, I bowed my head like I knew I should, closed my eyes tight, and searched for the words that would sound the most spiritual and genuine. Just when I figured out what to say, I felt Mani's hand go limp and snapped my eyes open. I don't know if she closed her eyes to join me in prayer or what, but the way the monitors rang out let me know it would be the last time she closed her eyes.

Not even five seconds later, a team of medical staff came rushing in and moved like they had rehearsed this scene a million times before. Ushering me to other side of the door, they ran through their usual resuscitation efforts while I stood in the hallway, still in shock. I knew I should stay put and wait to see the outcome, but my chest felt tight and my throat felt like it was gon' choke a nigga if I didn't get some fresh air ASAP. I jogged toward the elevator just as a couple was stepping off, mashing the button to get downstairs and outside to let this shit all sink in.

Mani was gone, like for real gone, and I had to be the one to fall through Ms. Pamela's house and tell her seed. *What the fuck did I sign up for?*

I didn't have a chance to think about an answer to my question because the elevator stopped three floors down, and when the doors slid open, I saw the last person I wanted to see, considering a nigga wasn't even halfway ready to face her and tell her what was up.

"Savage? What are you doing here?"

I was so shocked to see Bee's ass standing there that I couldn't even get my words together. Even though I hadn't done shit wrong, I knew the way she caught me off guard had a nigga lookin' guilty as hell.

"Oh, your ass on mute now, huh? See, this is the very reason I'm not fuckin' with your ass now! Lemme guess–"

"On some real shit, Beautiful, I can't even do this with you today."

"Do what? Nigga, ain't nobody thinkin' 'bout your ass! I was minding my damn business until–"

"Bee, chill."

"And fuck you! How 'bout that? You don't control my fuckin' mouth!"

"Yo, chill the fuck out!"

My voice boomed off the walls of the elevator as I closed the space between us and had her ass hemmed up in the corner.

"All that yellin' and shit ain't even necessary, real talk. I'm not with the shit today, so if you ain't got shit nice to say, just shut the fuck up and ride your ass down to wherever you got to be."

"Nigga, who the fuck—"

"Fall. The. Fuck. Back."

I guess she got the message that time because she didn't say shit else the rest of the way down, and when the car reached the first floor and opened, I didn't even look back at Beautiful as I walked as fast as I could without lookin' like a damn fool. I heard lil' TJ call out to me as I rushed past the waiting area, but all I could do was hit him with a lil' head nod and keep it movin'. I needed some air before I passed the fuck out!

"Bruh, I'm sorry to hear that shit. You good?"

"Man, hell nah I ain't good. How the fuck I'mma look in lil' dude's face and tell him his moms is gone? What the fuck did I agree to, my nigga?"

Linc hit my phone just as I made it to my ride, and I was grateful because after dealing with Bee's crazy ass, I needed some peace and calm.

"This is some heavy shit, no doubt, so lemme know if I can help. You know Moms is good with kids and shit. Where you at now, though? I'm headed that way now."

"Bruh, I gotta get the fuck away for a minute. Shit's been ill today. Need to get my head together and shit. I was two seconds from chokin' ya girl out just now and she don't even know it."

Linc knew my struggles with Beautiful's outta control ass, and he always had jokes and shit. Ain't shit funny about a chick that can go from domin' a nigga up with some A-1 head one second to tryin' to slice his sack off the next.

"Nigga, that's 'cause you love that ass." Linc chuckled. "I feel you, though. I'mma have Mique drop me off at the hospital and we'll get up later. Hit my line and let a nigga know what you need."

"No doubt."

Back in the eerie quiet of my ride, my mind drifted to I don't know where as I drove to who knows where. Death wasn't something that fazed me, and aside from Linc and his fam, I didn't even let myself get attached to other people enough to give a fuck when it came time to throw dirt on their asses. At least, that's what I thought I was doin' until the reality of Mani's situation set in for me a few weeks back. Mani was like the last link to my past, and even though a nigga was choked up and driving through blinding tears now, I felt the power of her words.

It's okay to let her in... but make sure you do right by her... you're a good dude... let her see that.

With all the shit I'd been through, and through all the fucked-up things I had to answer for, I learned one thing about life that just kept smackin' a nigga upside the head. A person could never know what was waiting around the corner; all they could do was keep it pushin' and take the corner, or fall back and retreat. I damn sure didn't see being responsible for someone else's seed in my future, but shit, if Mani was trustin' me to take on the responsibility of raisin' her lil' dude, then I couldn't do shit but step the fuck up and do right by the lil' nigga, just like I promised his mama I would.

You know what always interrupts a nigga when he's tryin' to get a minute to himself, right? The gotdamn phone, and when I answered the call after ignoring the caller the first two times, I instantly knew a nigga wasn't about to get no kinda break to grieve and get my fuckin' feelings together.

Shit!

Chapter Thirteen

Linc

On life, it seemed like Niq couldn't catch a fuckin' break from the bullshit that seemed determined to take her down since the day I first laid eyes on her sexy ass in Walgreens months ago. I felt like this shit was my fault because had I not been chasing behind Mique's ass and freezin' my nuts off out in Colorado, Niq wouldn't have been in that car alone on nobody's fuckin' back road for anyone to fuck with her. One thing I knew, though, was that someone's mama was gonna be pullin' out her black dress for this shit.

"Do you want me to come in with you?" Mique offered. I had a bangin' headache since about a half hour before we landed, so she volunteered to drive once we touched down. It worked out for the best, too, since I needed to head straight to the hospital.

"Nah, I'm good, I'll hit you when I'm done," I told her as I exited the car, waving to her as she pulled off on her way to our parent's house.

Mique had been quiet since we got to the airport in Denver, and I dismissed it as the weight of the shit she was involved in just weighing on her. Shit, I couldn't blame her because she had to look Pops in the face and run down how she let ridin' that nigga Kappo's dick pull her away from what she knew damn well should've been her priority: the business.

I stopped off into the waiting area and chopped it up with Bee for a hot minute before I headed up to the floor Niq's room was on. My lil' short stack was hyped as shit to see me, but the sadness in her eyes let me know she was well aware something wasn't right with her mama. I made a note to do some over the top kiddie shit for her to get her mind off things, hit Bee's lil' man with the special handshake Savage taught him, and made my way to the elevators, bracing myself for whatever I was about to see. I had the car to myself on the way up and as I rode in silence, it hit me that I still didn't know why the fuck Mique was in the hospital when I first touched down in Colorado. I'd find out, though.

Niq was wide awake, and her eyes met mine the second I stepped through the entrance to her room. The nurse had briefed me on the way in, and I'll be damned if I ain't have to put her advice to use right away.

"Shh shh, calm down, you gotta relax, ma. Breathe," I coached her.

Her eyes welled up for what looked like the umpteenth time that day as she struggled to suck in as much air as she could. Her spoiled ass wouldn't be able to talk for weeks? Yeah, a nigga was gonna take full advantage of that, as soon as we got her back home and further along in recovering.

Niq finally calmed herself and started scribbling away on the small board they gave her to communicate since she couldn't speak. I leaned closer and squinted while trying to make sense of what she wrote. I could tell her thoughts were coming to her faster than she could write.

"Short stack's fine. I saw her right before I came up."

She erased the board and rushed through her next message.

"Ma, you already know what it is, I got her. I got y'all. When you gon' realize that?"

Her thoughts were already on who was going to look after Essence while she was laid up, and like always, I didn't understand why the fuck she kept questioning some shit she should've already known the answer to. I'd give her a pass, though, considering her current state. Still, she would have to get her mind right and stop askin' me about my baby like I was some lame nigga or some shit.

Niq's marker was racing again, and her next message made me chuckle because I could hear her words as though she was speaking them instead of writing.

"Hell yeah, you look funny as shit, but a cute funny... like a chipmunk or something."

Why the fuck did I say that? I don't know if her ass was trying to laugh or cry, but whatever the fuck it was, she was 'bout to drown in her own damn saliva if she didn't calm that shit down.

"Ma, you gotta take it easy. Trust me, we'll have plenty of time to laugh it up once they take that half helmet off your face."

She threw an empty cup at me that time, which missed my head by a good foot and a half.

"And you still throw like a girl, but lemme ask you somethin'," I steered our conversation (if that's what you could call it) in a different direction. "You remember anything? You see anything that stood out right before..."

That marker went to work skating across her lil' board, but she paused midway, erased what she'd written so far, and started over. She wrote smaller this time, I guess so she could fit her complete thought on the small board. Shit, as much as Niq talked, she might need a board as big as her damn hospital bed to get all her thoughts out.

She finally finished and passed the board to me, and after I took a second to decipher a few words, I dug into my pocket for my phone, snapped a picture of what she'd written, and shot it to Savage in a picture message. I knew my boy was goin' through right now, but I also knew he'd wanna keep his mind occupied so he didn't get too deep off in his emotions, and he'd do that with work. Plus, he was just as ready to body the muthafuckas behind Niq's accident as I was — he didn't say it, but anything that involved catchin' bodies and gettin' revenge, my nigga was down for it.

I guess the meds they had Niq on started to kick in because the next thing I knew, she was knocked out and drooling as *The Haves and the Have Nots* was watching her from the TV. Now that I laid eyes on her and saw that Bee wasn't lyin' when she said Niq was okay, I felt a bit more at ease and ready get to my parent's house and chop it up with Pops about all the info I dug up while in Colorado.

It felt like the AC had kicked back on in the room, so I adjusted the blanket to cover Niq to keep her warm before kissing her forehead and making my exit. I left her a lil' note on her board, letting her know I'd get short stack home and call Promise to come through and help out for the next few days. Yet again, Niq was proving how much of a fighter she was, and that shit was so fuckin' sexy to me. This girl had been to hell and back long before she met me, yet she kept right on picking herself up and refused to give up. Niq deserved the world, and I planned to give it to her. She was gonna squash this lil' beef with Moms too, but we'd cross that bridge once I got her closer to a full recovery.

Just when I was about to give Mique's ass a break, her selfish ass proved exactly why I didn't like fuckin' with her sometimes. I stood down in the waiting area for a good hour, and her ass never showed up. I hit her phone over and over, and nothing. I had something for her ass, though.

I didn't wanna bother Savage since I knew he had shit to do to get Emani's affairs in order, so I had an Uber scoop me and take me out to my parent's spot.

"Linc, baby, you made it!"

Moms rushed to meet me the minute I stepped through the door, and I fell right into her arms. I loved this woman to life, and it felt good to see her after being away and freezing my ass off in Colorado. My stomach instantly started dancing at the aroma wafting through the house, and I felt like I could get full off the smell alone. Moms was a beast in the kitchen, and please believe, you better not even think about debating her on it!

"I know you didn't fly all this way and not bring my baby girl with you. Where's LaMique?"

"Whatchu mean? She ain't here?"

If this broad left my ass stranded at the hospital to go chase behind that nigga Kap—

"Son. Where's your sister?" Pops asked, making his way toward the foyer from his office in the back of the house. I held up a finger, signaling them both to hold on while I tried to hit Mique's line again.

Nothing. Straight to voicemail this time.

Just as I turned to speak to Pops, my phone went off in my hand and thinking it was Mique calling right back, I answered without looking to see who was calling.

"Yo, Mique?"

"Hey Linc, umm... I heard about Aniqa's accident and just wanted to see how she was doing," Paxton spoke.

I left my parents standing in the foyer and stepped down the hall to the family room to chop it up with Paxton for a few. We tried not to talk business around Moms as much as possible, mainly because we didn't want or need any lectures about how God wouldn't be pleased with this and that. I'd never call her a hypocrite to her face, but all I knew was she didn't question God's pleasure when Pops laced her with the finer things in life, courtesy of the business. That was a discussion for another time, though.

I picked Paxton's brain for a few about some of this shit Savage had been able to dig up, then turned the conversation back to Niq to gauge this nigga's reaction when I brought her up. I wasn't a fool, so I was sure the nigga still had a lil' crush on my girl; I just wanted to see if the nigga knew well enough to keep that shit under wraps out of respect. Lucky for him, he did, so he'd live to breathe another day.

"Is everything good with your sister, though?" Paxton asked just as I was about to end the call, and his question struck me as odd.

"What made you ask that?"

He fell quiet for a second, which struck me as even more odd.

"All bullshit aside, my dude, this ain't the time to be on no Hasbro shit. If you know some shit, speak the fuck up."

I wasn't gonna volunteer shit concerning Mique, but if the nigga felt he had something to share, it was open season.

"Well... I don't know if... shi—"

"Dawg, if you don't spit that shit out!"

I had a headache, hadn't slept good since I took that flight out to Colorado, felt like I was still thawing out, and my girl was laid up in the hospital, which meant a nigga would have desert dick for I don't know how long — I had zero patience at the moment.

"I think Tiara pocket-dialed me earlier and she... I think her and Kappo might have LaMique..."

Fuck! This shit can't be life!

Right after Paxton ran down all the info he had, I shot one of our tech guys a text to see what he could dig up on the number Tiara accidentally called Paxton from. I planned to hit Savage's line next because despite all the shit he was dealing with, we needed to get to this business, especially if Paxton was right and those muthafuckas were on some kidnapping shit with my sister. Savage beat me to it, though, and rang my line not too long after I finished the text to my tech guy.

"Yo."

"L, man this shit is wild! How the fuck both Richmond and Charlotte got hit earlier!" Savage reported.

"My nigga, please tell me you ain't sayin' what the fuck I think you're sayin'."

"Dead ass," he confirmed, making my stomach take a turn for the worse.

Savage ran down the info he had, and pissed as I was, it was a no-brainer that Kappo was behind the vaults being emptied at both locations. It was also no coincidence that the nigga chose to hit on Thursday, the day the vaults were emptied with the stacks of cash being loaded up for transport. Now that he knew we were up on game, this nigga Kappo was goin' balls to the wall wreaking havoc in our shit, but it was all good. Like the pro he was, the tech guy came through and hit me with the location he'd been able to pull from the number I gave him, which meant one thing: Kappo and Tiara were about to get some eternal daddy/daughter time before the sun came up tomorrow.

Chapter Fourteen

Aniqa

Powerless. Helpless. FRUSTRATED. That's how I felt lying in this hospital bed yet again. I swear I thought I was done having to deal with this type of stuff once I left Je'Marcus for good, but it was like I had a damn heat-seeking tracker implanted somewhere. Trouble just seemed to find me, and it was the kind that left my ass on the sick and shut in list — hence, my present situation.

Add to that the fact that I couldn't even open my mouth to do simple stuff like smile, yawn, cough, or sneeze and yeah, I was over it all. Don't get me wrong, I was abundantly thankful that God saw fit to bring me through yet another trying situation, but laying in this bed and watching the world pass me by required something I didn't have a whole lot of lately: patience.

I'd dealt with more than my fair share of hospital visits while I was with Je'Marcus, so I learned that nothing was 100% when it came to medical treatment. At best, doctors made educated guesses on the prognosis of a patient, so what if they got things wrong in my situation? What if I never walked again? I was finally in a place in my life where I could work on really getting myself together, really doing me, and this happens? Literally just started school.

Then, there was Linc. He was always telling me, *I got y'all*, and I heard him each time he said it, but did he really mean it? I knew he cared for Essie and even treated her like she was his own flesh and blood, but would he still be down for me if I never walked again? He'd already done so much for us, so the last thing I wanted to do was be a burden to him. Shit, what if I could never wipe my own ass again without being in pain? *Dammit!*

"Whoa, Aniqa, you okay?"

Like I'd been doing damn near every day, I got so deep off in my thoughts that I forgot my respirations were somewhat restricted by what Linc called a *half helmet.* His yellow ass stayed with jokes, but I had something for him, just as soon as I was back on my feet again.

"Come on, breathe with me," Paxton coached me, and all I wanted to do in that moment was scream.

I was beyond sick and tired of hearing people tell me to *calm down, breathe, take it easy.* I could barely feel my legs and had to work to breathe without feeling pain; I didn't see a damn thing to be calm about. Still, I did what I knew I needed to do because the thought of choking to death wasn't pleasant.

I pointed as best I could at the pitcher of iced water the nurse dropped off just as Paxton had arrived, hoping he could read my nonverbals and understand my request. Like the sweetheart he was, he sprang into action and helped me take a few sips to sate my thirst and soothe the itchiness that never seemed to leave my throat. Once I'd pulled myself together, I nodded my thanks and did my best to readjust my upper body into a more comfortable position.

"You don't have to thank me... you don't owe me anything, Aniqa. I'm just glad to see that you're okay."

Paxton fell silent and watching him slip off into his thoughts, I was reminded of when we first met, and of the great friendship we used to have. It's not that we weren't friends anymore, but I don't know, things sort of changed once Linc and I really got serious about one other. Paxton was infatuated with me from day one, and I knew his feelings were genuine since I was far from eye-catching back then. I had a small wardrobe that consisted of a few pieces I tried to recycle and re-purpose to make as many outfits as possible, and I might have had two pairs of shoes to switch out for work. Je'Marcus wouldn't hesitate to lay hands on me if he thought I was trying to *look good for the next dude*, so I kept my look as plain Jane as possible; no makeup, and just enough effort with my hair to make it look like I hadn't just rolled out of bed.

Basic was exactly how I looked back then, but that didn't stop Paxton from making sure I felt like the prettiest girl in the world whenever I was in his presence. He was definitely one of the good ones, even made life bearable back then, and I knew I was lucky to still have him around because good friends – genuine friends that wanted nothing in return but your friendship – were hard to find. Especially male ones.

Paxton was still sitting there quietly, but it was almost a sad quiet, so I did my thing and scribbled out my inquiry to pick his brain. He finally pulled himself away from his thoughts and did his best to read my chicken scratch before replying.

"I just feel so horrible that this happened to you, Niq. Just makes me think about... you're such a good person, a lot better than most people. I know I don't even deserve your understanding, but just know I'm glad you found it in your heart to forgive me."

I thought I was giving him a deep frown and staring muthafuckly at him, but I don't think that's what my face displayed because he kept right on talking like we were on the same page, and man, the words that fell from his lips next? Let's just say I felt like I'd been hit AGAIN, but by a tractor trailer this time.

"I had no idea what I was agreeing to, Aniqa, and by the time I found out what was going on, it was too late... I couldn't look into Essence's eyes and not see you. I knew I fucked up, like majorly fucked up, and I just couldn't do it... so I... I dropped her at the closest place that I knew was safe. Aniqa, you gotta know I'd never hurt you or Essence, never, and I promise I made sure she was okay the whole time. I just got caught up..."

Pause. Was this dude saying what I think he was saying?

Paxton opened his mouth to say something else, but never got the chance because in walked who? Linc. See, one of the hardest parts about being tied and wired to this damn bed was that I couldn't reach out and touch people when I wanted to. I just had to take shit lying down — literally.

So many things came together in my head all at once, and when I locked eyes with Linc, my gut told me that he had some explaining to do. Every time I brought up the subject of Essence's kidnapping, it felt like Linc tried to redirect my attention, almost like he didn't want to talk about it. Almost like he knew more than he was telling me.

Paxton must have picked up on the mood shift in the room because he whispered another apology, gave my hand a squeeze, said he'd check in with me later to see how I was doing, and made his exit. Linc gave him a nod as he left, then came over to take Paxton's place in the chair next to my bed, and you know I had something waiting for him, right?

I felt my hand cramping up from the tight grip I had on the marker as I furiously scrawled out a question that, judging by his reaction, Linc had been dreading. He stood there with his eyes slightly bucked, so I pushed through the pain and made sure my face sent exactly the message I intended this time. I tapped the dry erase marker against the board, stopping on each word for emphasis. Best version of shouting I could do for now.

"Pshhh..." He blew out a long breath and dragged his hand from his forehead down to his chin, something he always did when he was about to go into a deep discussion. "Lemme explain, Niq."

My hand was already on the move, erasing my previous message and scrawling another one by the time he finished speaking.

"I did, but lemme explain," he offered a response to my question. I didn't need to hear an explanation, though, not shit else. This man knew who had taken my baby and didn't tell me. That's all I needed to know.

"Shit, ma..."

Shit is right, and that's exactly what I had for him. Not shit.

"There's a lot to the story, ma, and it's not always a quick and clean fix. I'mma handle it though, bet that. There's a method to the madness, just know that."

Know that hell. Essie was snatched. We now knew who took her. They needed to pay. End of story, right? Seemed like a quick, clean fix to me.

"Look, there's a lot more shit goin' on that you don't even know about, and as bad as I wanna get at that bitch Tiara, I had to let some other shit fall into place first. That's done now, and you got my word I'll take care of her. Now Paxton, well, let's just say ya boy got a pass because he's more valuable alive than dead with all the shit we got goin' on."

Again, my hand was on the move because I now needed to know what the hell Tiara had to do with the whole situation.

"It looks like ol' girl was behind it, yes, and like I said, I'll take care of her. That's not even something you need to worry about. You focus on gettin' up outta here."

Did I say I felt helpless? One of the things I had to deal with from Je'Marcus was always being the last to know about shit. They kept me on a need to know basis in that house, and it seemed like there wasn't a whole lot of shit they felt I needed to know. I refused to live like that again, to be treated like a child that needed to go sit in a corner and mind her business. I damn sure wasn't about to be excluded from anything concerning a child I gave birth to, and Linc knew that shit. It was all good, though, because if he wasn't prepared to deal with Tiara's ass, I knew someone who was.

"I know what your lil' ass is thinking, and you can dead that shit. We already have somethin' in motion to take care of her ass, and a lot of other muthafuckas too, so y'all stay your Charlie's Angels asses outta this and let us handle it. Bee's wild ass won't do shit but get in our way, so don't even stir her ass up. I keep tellin' you that I got you, so let me have you, Niq. Trust that," he finished, pulling his eyes away from me for a second to check his phone.

Fuck what he said. I was definitely gonna tell Beautiful about this shit, and may the chips fall wherever...

They say be careful what you ask for because you just might get it, and I was living that very thing right now. I passed whatever neurological tests the doctors needed to see favorable performance on, confirming there was sufficient function in my lower body to move forward with physical therapy when it was time. With favorable chances for a full recovery and a ton of pain meds, I was now resting in the comfort of our home and, more importantly, back with my little Essie. However, it came at a price, and that price was being in a confined space with Linc and being forced to look upside his head damn near all day. I understood his care and concern, and I even appreciated him trying to juggle work and family stuff while trying to be around for me, especially after he told me what was going on with his sister. I still couldn't stand the sight of his ass right now, though, and I wanted to swing on him every time he came within a foot of me. I guess the silver lining in the situation was that I couldn't speak to him, which meant I could low-key ignore him.

This man watched me basically fall apart when Essence was snatched, watched me feel like I couldn't eat or sleep because my baby was gone, saw me fall into fits of hopelessness because I just knew Je'Marcus had taken her to try to get back at me for finally finding the courage to leave him, and not once did he even think to let me know he found out who took her. I couldn't help but look at him in a different light now because he swore he was down for us, swore we were building a family, yet he was allowing whomever was involved in Essie's kidnapping to walk around free and clear? Of course, Beautiful hit the roof when I let her know, and I instantly felt bad because the last thing she needed was another reason to be in conflict with Savage, especially after the bomb she told me he'd dropped on her.

"Helloooo? You hear lil' mama talkin' to you, don't ignore her."

Linc leaned over and snapped his fingers in my face with a little too much bass in his voice for my liking. Honestly, I didn't hear Essence and wouldn't dare ignore her after I just went what felt like forever without being able to really spend time with her. I rolled my eyes at Linc so hard it felt like they'd get stuck, then turned my attention to the book Essence was trying to show me. It was one of those interactive activity books that helped kids learn sight words and work on pronunciation. She went through two full sentences without having to use the pen to "help" her pronounce the word, and I fought the smile that would only cause pain with my jaw wired shut.

My baby had come such a long way, from not talking at all to being a little social butterfly, and I was so happy to see her thriving. She was the one good thing that came from that toxic existence I had with Je'Marcus.

"You can have your lil' attitude all you want, but you'll still need me to help you wash that ass at the end of the day," Linc joked as he got up to let my mother in so he could head out and tend to some business.

"You say bad word!" Essie called him out. She was little Ms. Profanity Patrol, and it almost seemed like she listened extra hard to make sure she didn't miss anything. Kids.

Linc made his exit, thankfully, and I was left with another person that was mildly annoying: my mother. Again, I appreciated having her help and was glad she was here to spend time with Essie, but I just wanted to be left alone, didn't want to be bothered.

"Okay baby, you have strawberries, mangoes, pineapples, bananas, peaches, and kiwi in here. Which do you want me to blend with your yogurt? Oh wait, you had strawberries and kiwi yesterday, so how about mango and banana today?" Promise called from the kitchen.

"Look Mommy, I do it! I do it!" Essie shrieked.

See what I mean? Not a minute to damn myself.

Chapter Fifteen

Beautiful

Wanna know the main reason I stayed in the frame of mind to chin check these lying ass niggas? Because they were LIARS. Full of alternative facts and half-truths, and then when the full truth came out, they had the nerve to look upside your head like you had two noses or some shit when you called them out. That's exactly how Savage was looking at me right now, and Lord knows that if we weren't in a public park with kids around, I would've done my best to make his ass feel my wrath. The only thing I asked this nigga to do was be real with me, all cards face up, no surprises. Was that too much to ask?

"You gon' let me explain or nah?"

Dumb questions. I hated those too. Lyin' ass niggas with dumb ass questions. Like nigga, I'm sittin' here and you're still breathing, so what the fuck? TALK!

"Bee—"

"How 'bout this. You don't even waste those words you're about to use to lie to my fuckin' face, and I'll wipe your sorry ass face from my memory and act like I never met you. Deal?"

"Gotdamn, Beautiful, can you shut the fuck up and just listen?"

"Nigga, I don't know who the fuc–"

"You, I'm tryin' to talk to you and let you know what's up if you let a nigga get more than a few words out. Shit! So, how 'bout this? You sit there, shut the fuck up, and listen to what a nigga gotta say. Deal?"

We had to be due for a full blue moon or some shit because you know what? I actually shut the hell up and let his ass talk! Ain't that some shit?

"Aight, so check it. I got some heavy shit to lay out, but I need to get all this shit out before you even respond. Can you let me do that?"

Nodding my agreement, I crossed one leg over the other, got as comfortable as I could on the stiff ass park bench, and gave Savage my undivided attention. I had a feeling this shit was about to be good.

I don't know what I thought was about to come out his mouth, but I do know that I wasn't prepared for the quick history lesson that he laid out for me. I guess he'd learned enough to know if some shit sounded half ass, I was bound to hit him with a million and one questions, so he literally started from the first day he and Emani met. He even touched on the shit leading up to his arrest and time incarcerated, which was something he rarely talked about. I knew enough to know that he'd ended someone's life, but unlike the type of shit TJ's father was involved in, Savage's crime seemed to be justified, for the most part.

By the time Savage had wrapped up his explanation, I was speechless. He was doing his best not to get choked up when he spoke of Emani's passing, and I realized that no matter how much I flipped on him, no matter how many times I told him to leave me the fuck alone, I had nothing but respect for this man. The fact that she trusted him to do right by her child meant he probably was a good dude. Shit, I hoped so, but you know I was still gonna have my questions, right?

He took a deep breath when he was done, then shifted his posture to get a better view of me. I just sat there quiet, though, still letting everything soak in as I turned my body to face the playground equipment where TJ and Essie were running back and forth. I know I was quiet for a good, solid two minutes before I finally spoke.

"So, what now?" I stared straight ahead, body stiff as I

tried to ease into the lightweight line of questioning I'd been holding in while he spoke.

"What now is I'm a man of my word."

I was anything but calm on the inside, but I did my best to keep my face stiff and contain my emotions. Some of the most difficult shit I'd ever had to do. I really did wanna hold shit together and, for once, have a heart to heart talk with Savage without all the rah-rah shit, but see, the way my mouth was set up....

"I mean, what you're doing it's a good thing, but why you?"

"The hell you mean by that?"

"What I mean is this—why would she expect you, of all people, to take on the responsibility of raising her kid? Lemme ask you something, and I promise if you lie to me, you're dead to me from this very moment forward."

"Shoot it."

Savage's brow bent in a furrow of aggravation, almost like he just knew I was about to come out my face with some bullshit. I can't even lie; I probably would have under normal circumstances, but this really was some heavy shit that he'd laid in my lap.

"Are you his father?"

"Man, I told you I ain't got no kids, Bee. The fuck would I lie about that for?"

"I'm just asking, Savage. Shit, chicks don't just go around giving their kids to random niggas..."

"Which part of what I ran down did you not hear? How I'mma be somebody's daddy when the lil' nigga was both conceived and born while I was locked up?"

I got quiet again, took a deep breath, then did a quick scan to make sure the kids were still within my line of sight before resituating my posture on the bench. I turned to look Savage dead in the eye this time, because I needed to be able to see through to his soul when he answered this next question.

"You still love her, don't you?"

I could tell I caught him off-guard, but I couldn't even act like it wasn't a legit question that had been floating around in my head for a while now. Savage wasn't exactly the overly affectionate, lovey dovey type, so for him to be walking around still caring about a chick from his past, I knew there had to be some sort of feelings there. I was far from stupid, and I needed to make sure he knew that.

Seeing him just sit there without even making an effort to

answer my question, I gave him a little disclaimer because something told me he was about to feed me some bullshit to avoid a confrontation.

"I need you to promise me something, Savage, and I'm dead ass serious about this shit. Don't keep shit else from me. Don't lie to me. I don't believe in that *lying to protect my feelings* shit. I can get lies from any bum ass nigga on the street. The least you can do is be straight up with me. I give you that, so I expect it in return."

Voice now tinged with a hint of aggravation, I did my best not to get any louder than I already was. I really wasn't trying to blow up in these folks' park, but at the same time, I wasn't about to let this nigga mistake my patience to hear his explanation for my being gullible enough to accept some random line of bullshit. I'd pretty much been an open book with him, so if we had any hope of moving forward from this uncomfortable ass bench, I needed him to give me that same thing in return.

"Love her? Yes, but let me explain," he began. Oh yeah, this nigga had my full attention now, and this shit better make sense.

"Mani was the only real shit in my life for so long, so of course, I'm always gon' have love for her. In love with her? No. The fact that she trusted me to raise her seed as my own? That's love, and I can't do shit but respect it. But understand this, she ain't got shit to do with you and me."

Part of me wanted to give him credit for doing what I asked and being honest, but the other part wanted me to snatch his face off for talking about loving another chick, rest her soul in peace. I don't think I had anything against Emani *personally* since she'd never done anything to me, but still. I just couldn't see how this nigga would ever be able to develop any type of real feelings for me if he was still stuck on her, and please believe, he was still stuck on her. I could see it all up and through his face when he spoke of her.

"Don't even look at me like that, ma. I ain't got shit to lose by keeping it a buck with you, no reason to do anything less at this point. I know that shit might not be what you wanna hear, but shit, I'm not 'bout to sit here and lie either. It is what it is, and it ain't something I can change, so you either gon' rock with a nigga or fall back."

You know what my ass did, right?

"TJ! Essie! Let's go!"

"So, I guess it's good that his ass was honest with me and told me everything, but I'm still stuck on the fact that he didn't tell me sooner."

I couldn't think of anyone else who would sit there and listen to my bipolar feelings about Savage without judging me, and even though Aniqa couldn't verbally respond, I knew I could still count on her to give me that sisterly type of feedback that I so desperately needed in this situation.

I leaned forward, tucked my right leg under my body, and sunk even deeper into the plushness of Linc and Niq's couch. She scribbled away on her little board, waiting until I was good and settled before she flashed it in my direction.

"I'm not about to let this nigga have me out here looking stupid, Niq. Fuck all that. And how the fuck do you compete with a dead chick?"

Niq's marker raced across the board, scrawling out her sentiments of how silly I was being, iterating that there was nothing and no one to be in competition with.

"Okay, so let's say I put all that shit to the side. This nigga basically has a whole son now. Where will he fit into all this?"

The same place YOUR son fits into all this, crazy! You expect him to accept TJ, you need to do the same.

Niq was right, and I couldn't do shit but sit there quietly because I never even stopped to look at it that way. Savage didn't even think twice about accepting the fact that I had a kid, and he was so good with him. Maybe things would work out. But damn...

"Niq, how the hell are we supposed to have anything real if his heart is somewhere else? He straight admitted to me that he loved the chick! What the hell am I supposed to do with that?"

Realize he's trying to give YOU his heart and accept it.

Again, my girl had me silent as I let her words marinate for a minute. Now that I knew the reason why he'd been kinda off lately, I couldn't say there was really anything Savage had been dishonest about. Damn sure couldn't deny that I missed having him around, so maybe I should just let go and see where things went.

I figured Niq was about to co-sign my almost-decision because her marker was back at work twerking across the board, but when she held it up for me to read, my mind jumped the tracks and completely switched gears.

"Oh, hell no! I got something for that bitch!"

Chapter Sixteen

Savage

When Bee called and asked to meet up at the park, I felt like that shit was a setup at first. She wasn't exactly the type to A - admit she was wrong or B - apologize and meet up on some kumbaya shit. I knew shit was gon' either go all the way right, or all the way left. Either way, I had some shit I needed to lay out for her, and I knew there was no point in puttin' that shit off.

I was neither spiritual nor religious, but I figured God was lookin' out for a nigga because Beautiful did something I ain't even know she was capable of: sat down, shut the fuck up, and actually listened to a nigga. It felt good layin' all that shit out for her. I heard Mani's words ringing in my head the whole time, so I said '*fuck it?*' and decided to let her in, really let her get close to a nigga. Females were quick to chase after a bad boy, but when it came time to be forgiving and see past a nigga's flaws, that was a whole 'nother story. There wasn't a day that went by that I didn't think about the first time I took a life—which I did my time for—but you know what? I'd do the shit again in a heartbeat. Nothing was more important than family, so I'd catch as many bodies as necessary to protect the ones I loved.

"This butter soft ass muthafucka just had to go and run his damn mouth. Now, I know I ain't gon' hear the end of this shit from Niq."

Linc was pacing back and forth like some hot shit was about to go down, and I guess it was in a way—just as soon as we ran up on that nigga, Kappo, and his scandalous ass daughter.

"Bruh, I don't even think the lil' nigga meant to harm by it, but you right. He ain't have to blow ya spot up like that. Don't even stress that shit, though. We get this shit lined up and handle up like we plan to, and we'll dead that issue by default, feel me?"

Linc half-nodded as he tended to a notification that had just buzzed through on his phone. My mind was working overtime doing a mental calculation of all the shit we needed to handle so we could finally get somewhere, sit the fuck down, and just enjoy being able to wake up without heavy shit hanging over our heads. Just when I was about to light up and blow some of those exotic trees from Linc's family business...

Tap Tap Tap

Linc slid my patio door open to greet our interruption.

"What's good, lil' man?"

"I can't r-reach the s-shower thing..." Mani's son, Dre, spoke just above a whisper.

He'd been pretty quiet since the first night we got back to my spot, and I wasn't sure if that stuttering thing he did was just from being sad about losing his moms, or if he had a legit speech impediment. I made a note to find out how we could get it checked out and get him whatever help he needed because shit, kids were bad as fuck nowadays, and I didn't know how I could handle lil' man coming home and telling me someone was fuckin' with him.

Coming home. Felt strange as fuck thinkin' 'bout a kid *coming home* to my spot, but on some real shit, it made a nigga feel all warm and shit inside knowing I never had to come home to an empty house again.

"Everything straight?" Linc hit me when I stepped back out onto the patio after helping Dre get the shower started.

"'Bout as straight as can be, bruh. Seem like it's a lot of shit I don't know shit about, so I'm wingin' this shit as I go, feel me?"

"No doubt. Just keep him fed, clothed, and happy and you can't fail," Linc offered before downing the last of his cranberry juice. "You and Bee good, though?"

"Bruh, I don't even know what the fuck is what when it comes to her. Shit, a nigga tried to do the right thing and come clean, now it seems like she ain't fuckin' with a nigga in no way, shape, or form. Ain't even cussin' a nigga out, and I guess I'm a fucked-up nigga because I miss that shit."

True story. Crazy as it sounds, even when Bee was screamin' at me, that shit felt good because I knew I had her attention. Just hearing her voice start to climb those octaves when she called herself turnin' up made my dick brick up like some on-demand shit.

"Nah, you're not a fucked-up nigga. You're an in-love nigga!"

Linc sat there with his feet kicked up, laughing that shit up like it was the funniest thing ever.

"Nigga, fuck all that love shit. I ain't got time to do shit else but get to this business and hope I don't fuck up too bad with lil' man in there. Lil' nigga asked me to mail a letter he wrote for Mani to heaven the other day. How the fuck do I respond to that shit?"

"Damn, bruh...that's some deep shit."

"No doubt. I'm feelin' the shit outta Bee, but I got too much on my plate to be chasing after her emotionally unstable ass, feel me?"

"Bipolar. You can say it."

"Shit, that too. All I know is a nigga ain't built to handle that shit if I'm not able to take that shit out on her pussy later. She start fuckin' a nigga again and I'll see what I can do. That shit gotta balance itself out somehow. Anyway, nigga, what's the move for tomorrow?"

Talkin' about shit between me and Bee had my head throbbing, so I needed to switch gears and talk about some shit where I could get the other kinda release I needed.

"Daddy day care for your ass, nigga."

Laughing at my expense again, Linc shot off another quick text. His lil' jab reminded me that I needed to get up with Mani's neighbor, Ms. Pamela, to see if she could keep Dre for me while we made this move to get Mique back. She'd been nice enough to keep him for me a few times so far, but I didn't wanna wear out the welcome. Plus, I knew I needed to get a more permanent type of arrangement in place for him. A nigga had to work, and with Bee iggin' my ass, it wasn't like I could lean on her for a lil' help.

"What's good, Pops?" Linc answered his incoming call, switched the phone to speaker, and laid it on my patio table.

"Change of plans for tomorrow. My lawyer just called and

said we have a meeting with the DA at 10 a.m."

"Shit, you know what for?" Linc frowned while pressing his Pops for more info.

"Lawyer said they were tight-lipped. Just asked that we be there and said it couldn't wait."

"Aight, so I'll have Savage head to the spot in Charlotte while I ride with you and—"

"Not even necessary. You two go ahead and head out as planned. Tending to that situation is non-negotiable. I'll give you a call as soon as we find out what they want and let you know where we go from there," Big Linc instructed, and though his face said he wanted to do anything but, Linc gave his pops his agreement before they changed the topic.

"You two ready to move on that other situation?"

"No doubt. Head out in a few."

"Everybody in position?" Big Linc continued.

"Yup."

"Exactly what I like to hear. Dead this shit tonight, son. I hate to lay my head to rest for the night knowing I lied to your mother. This cannot be an issue when the sun comes up."

Linc's pops had always been a man of few words; rarely

even cursed, so when he *did* curse, you knew someone was about to take their last breath. He didn't even have to come out and say he was pissed with Linc for letting Mique get snatched up. The ragged timbre of his voice said it all, and the way he spoke with finality made one thing clear: Linc better get to Mique in time, or Big Linc would be all over his ass.

"I got you, Pops."

"And son? Bring my baby girl home in one piece," Big Linc finished before ending the call.

"Bruh, why you look like a two-year old that just pissed on himself when Big Linc be gettin' in that ass?

"Fuck you, nigga. Let's go get this shit over with."

That nigga Linc hated being called out on shit, so I laughed to myself as he huffed his way past me and back into the living room.

Lucky for me, Linc was able to talk his parent's housekeeper into falling through and keeping an eye on Dre for me so we could step out. She didn't know Mique was missing either, and we planned to keep it that way because if she got wind of what was really up, she'd burn up the phone lines letting Linc's mom know what the deal was.

"Nigga, are you gonna tuck lil' man in and say

goodnight?" Linc frowned as we headed to the front door.

"Shit, I gotta do that too?"

I told you, all this parental responsibility shit was new to me. I made sure lil' man was fed and bathed for the night. There was more to this shit?

Leaving Linc standing in the living room, I headed back to what used to be my guest room, trying to think of what I'd seen Bee do to put her lil' dude down for the night.

"Ay lil' man, you good?" I peeked my head into the room before entering, then took a knee next to the bed.

"Y-yes, b-but can I have some water?"

Man, we had to do something about this soft ass voice of his. A man needed to have some bass in his voice. I was gon' get him right, though.

"Hold up, you ain't gon' piss in my bed, are you?" I joked, trying to lighten the mood and help lil' man relax a little. We were still getting used to each other, so there was still some awkwardness that we had to push through.

The smile he flashed in return damn near had my jaw on the floor. He was the spitting image of Emani when he smiled.

"I'm n-not a b-baby, Sam." He giggled, brushing his locs

out of his face as he turned over onto his side. His stutter had him stuck every time he tried to say my full name, so I told him he could call me Sam for the time being.

"Damn right. You a man, aight? Lemme hear you say it."

"I'm a m-man," he mumbled.

"Nah, say it like you mean it, lil' man," I coached.

"I'm a m-man," he sounded off a little louder.

"That's what's up." We bumped fists as I stood, but he stopped me before I could make my exit.

"C-can you p-pray with me? M-momma said I gotta s-say my p-prayers every night, but I don't l-like sayin' 'em b-by myself."

Here we go with this prayer thing again. I didn't know the first thing about prayin' with a kid, so I hoped lil' man took the lead. Sure enough, he stumbled his way through what I could tell was a prayer Mani probably taught him.

"S-say Amen, Sam," he called me out when he finished and I didn't speak up.

"My bad, lil' man. Amen. You good?" I asked one last time as I got up from my knees. Felt good havin' someone need my presence to help 'em get settled in for the night.

"Y-yes."

"Aight, cool. I gotta step out right quick, but Ms. Sheree is right in the next room if you need anything."

He nodded his understanding and giving him one last fist bump, I dimmed the dome light and pulled his door shut. Found out the first night he was afraid of the dark, so I left the light on a dim setting until I could get him a lil' night light or something.

"You good, Pops?" Linc clowned when I reappeared in the living room.

"Nigga, you the one with a whole wife and kid, so you can't say shit."

"Damn right, them my babies and I dare a muthafucka to say otherwise."

"Aight killa, bring your ass on so we can go get Mique before Big Linc gotta put his foot up your ass," I joked, hitting Ms. Sheree with a head nod to let her know I was heading out. She was in the kitchen putting a pie in the oven. Where she got the shit to make it was beyond me because I ain't have shit up in my fridge or cabinets suitable for making a damn pie.

I knew I still had some ways to go, but I could honestly say that for the first time since I moved into my spot, it felt like a home instead of just where I lived. Amazing what how much a kid could change your life.

"One in front, one in back. Nothing on the sides, but there's nothing but open space, so we gotta be quick with that shit since we won't have any cover," one of lil' niggas in the crew we called up explained. Linc told these muthafuckas to dress incognito and what does this nigga show up in? All black outfit and skully with a bright ass, lime green logo. The fuck?

"They got her yoked up in a room toward the back, down in the basement. Ain't seen nobody go in since they locked her in there, though," one of the other niggas explained, passing a set of binoculars to Linc so he could get a view of the door leading to the room where they were holding Mique. Looked like he followed directions and had an unfair advantage. This nigga's flesh was so dark, you couldn't tell where the fabric ended and the skin on the back of his hand began. I ain't know what the lil' nigga's real name was, but he was officially dubbed Black in my book.

"So, what's the move, boss man?" nigga #3 asked, adjusting his vest and holster like he was ready to get it in, lookin' like an off-brand super trooper or some shit.

"We go in there and get her, then blow this muthafucka, that's what."

As far as I was concerned, this nigga Kappo and his lil' thot ass daughter had stirred up enough shit and hit one too many licks at our expense. Shit was crazy when you thought about it, because it ain't like them muthafuckas were the smartest people. They were just sneaky as fuck. Either way, I didn't appreciate nobody making a fool out of me and mine, so I was ready to dead all this shit for good.

"Aight, here." Lime Green passed me and Linc a few earpieces. "We got a few cameras in place. No sound, though, but at least we can see what's what and give y'all a head's up if need be. I estimate we got a good five minutes before Big Swole at the front leaves to make his rounds and check everything out."

"What about the nigga at the back?" Linc frowned.

"Nigga been in the same spot since we got here. Ain't moved," Black explained.

"Aight cool, so five minutes. Let's get–" Linc confirmed, but was cut off.

"Shit! The camera feed just went down," Super Trooper fussed.

"Well, get that muthafucka back!" Linc's voice boomed,

sounding more and more like his pops.

"I'm...I'm tryin', but this is all I get." Lime Green showed us the screen on his tablet, which showed some shit about a DNS error. "Looks like they somehow intercepted the feed and disrupted the signal."

"Man, fuck all this technical gadget shit. We gon' get down like we got down before every nigga and his mama had a fuckin' smartphone. Get in, stay low, move fast, and get the fuck out. Feel me?"

Sometimes, I felt like Linc got so swept up in how we did big things now that he forgot how we started out, and how Big Linc used to make us put in work to prove we were built for the kinda shit he was trying to groom Linc to step into.

"Aight, let's get this shit over with. A nigga got shit to do," Linc gave the order for us to move out, and we did just that.

Sixty seconds later, we'd managed to slip through a ground floor window and clear the main hallway with no issues. A brief nod and a few hand signals, and Linc and I were moving in opposite directions. I headed to handle the big nigga at the front while Linc made his way down to the room where the crew said Mique was being held.

I took one last glance to make sure Linc was good, then whipped around and was greeted with what felt like a set of brass knuckles trying to rearrange my face.

"Shit!"

Apparently, Big Swole heard me coming and moved surprisingly swift for a morbidly obese muthafucka. Them big ones fall hard, though, so I rushed his legs and threw him off his feet. His body crashed to the floor just as what sounded like a convoy of AK-47s rang out.

"Fuck these niggas come from!" I shouted to...shit...myself since I was pretty sure Linc was well outta earshot.

If I made it out of this shit alive, I knew one thing. I was gon' kill me three additional muthafuckas for the half ass recon and surveillance they did. This was exactly why I said all niggas weren't 'bout this life. Niggas had expert proficiency on Call of Duty and the shit had 'em thinkin' they were fit for some real-life type shit. Fortunately, a nigga always packed for situations like this, and I had more than a lil' aggression I needed to unload.

One by one, I managed to take out three bodies that just a few seconds earlier, were bustin' from upstairs. One by one, their bodies fell to rest a few inches short of my feet. A nigga's chest swelled with pride, but my celebration was cut short when...

"Ahhhhhhhhhhh, fuck!"

Shit! Was my nigga Linc was hit! Damn, this shit went way the fuck left! How the fuck—

BOOM!

It felt like the whole wall came crashin' in on a nigga. All I know is whatever the fuck it was, the shit knocked me off my feet, laid me out on my back, and had the air so thick with all kinda dust and debris that I had to pull my shirt up over my mouth to breathe.

"Get down! Don't move!"

"South entrance clear!

I didn't know if I was hearin' shit in the same room with me or across some kinda radio, but what I DID know is it sounded like the law had run up in this shit. Now the question is, who the fuck were they here for?

"West side all clear!"

"East side is clear as well!"

My mind was screamin' for me to get my ass up and see what was going on, but shit, I felt like I was pinned to the dank coldness of the subfloor. No tile, no wood flooring— straight subfloor.

I finally found the strength to pull myself up onto my forearms, and that's when I saw what looked like the same jeans and boots Linc was wearing, stretched out across the floor.

"What the fuck! Linc!"

Adrenaline pumping so hard my veins were jumping, I pulled myself up into a kneeling position, then slowly rose to my feet, only to be met with a sharp jab of steel square between my shoulder blades.

"Yo—"

"Hands up, and stay right where you are!"

"Mannnn, what the fuck? I ain't did shit!"

"Hands up or I'll lay your ass out! Now!"

I wasn't new to this shit, and being that we were in some old, dusty ass building, way deep off in the middle of rural Surry County, I knew just how this shit would go. It was a picture-perfect setting for some over eager ass cop to lay some niggas down and swear they thought they were reaching for a taser and ended up with a Glock. I didn't have a bunch of family to riot and protest in the streets, but I wasn't tryin' to become the next face on a #BlackLivesMatter t-shirt either, so you know what my ass did? Got the fuck back down so this clown didn't have even the slightest reason to put no lead in my ass.

"All clear back on the North side!"

The cop's radio crackled with one last status report, confirming they'd secured the building. Out of the corner of my eye, I could see some movement back where Linc headed down to get Mique earlier, then a figure emerged and entered the hallway.

"Jason?" LaMique spoke as soon as she made out the figure standing over me through the thin smokiness left behind by the flash grenade. She started walking in his direction, but froze when her eyes came to rest on what lay at her feet.

"Oh God! Linc!" Mique rushed and fell to her knees at Linc's side. "No! Savage! What happened? Somebody call for help, please!" she pleaded.

I guess Mique's acknowledgement was proof enough that I wasn't part of what or whomever the hell the law came to bust because the clown, who I now knew was some nigga named Jason, let me up and moved over to where Mique kneeled next to her brother. *Wait, how the fuck did Mique know this damn cop's name?*

Three more officers poured into the room as the nigga, Jason, radioed for medical help for Linc. I caught a quick glimpse of the side of his face, and that's when it hit me. This Jason was the *same* Jason that worked at Big Linc and Linc's spot out in Colorado. But this nigga was a damn fed?

"H-how did you know—" Mique began, but he cut her off.

"Are you alright?" Jason turned toward Mique, helping her up to her feet as two of the other officers tended to Linc.

Mique was no good, though. She was physically there, but her eyes went blank for a second, almost like she'd mentally checked out. I ain't know if God was mad or tryin' to teach us all a lesson or what. In the span of a hot minute, Niq had been run off the road, Mique had been kidnapped, Emani passed away, I inherited a whole kid and shit, Linc was laid the fuck out unconscious, the nigga Jason turned out to be a fed, and Bee still wasn't fuckin' with a nigga.

There was a silver lining in all this bullshit, though. Two of the bodies resting a few feet away? None other than Kappo's snake ass and that dusty ass bitch, Tiara. Checkmate, bitches!

Chapter Seventeen

Linc

On everything I love, if I didn't see the inside of a hospital for another ten years, that would still be too damn soon. All a nigga was supposed to do was roll out, fall through and snatch Mique up, lay Kappo and Tiara's fraud asses to rest, and get Mique home before Moms woke up the next morning and realized she still hadn't come home. Fate had other plans for us all, though.

"Mr. Carmichael, your films confirm my initial diagnosis. You've suffered a grade 2 concussion, but I expect you to make a full recovery with no serious lasting effects," this cute lil' doctor explained, flashing a warm smile as she glanced back and forth between me and the chart she cradled in her hand.

"And your leg, let's see...looks like it's just a flesh wound, and I see my nurse has you all cleaned and bandaged up, so you're good to go with that as well. You'll want to change the bandage at least twice a day, or more often as needed," she continued, her face set in a pensive expression of concentration. Clearly, she was in her element tending to handsome patients such as myself, and I felt at ease knowing I had a qualified professional providing such a great bedside manner.

"Now, as far as your concussion, you'll want to take it easy for the next few weeks. Even if you start to feel better, you still need to relax and lighten your mental load as much as possible. As much as you can, avoid high-cognitive function mental activities such as reading, texting, doing pretty much anything on a computer, and even watching TV. If you have to do any of those things, I'd recommend not doing so for more than a few minutes at a time. Think you can do that?" The doctor smiled, flashing a straight, pristine set of pearly whites that looked like they were individually set in her pretty little head.

"Doc, all due respect, I got things to do. I can't be laid up like some helpless charity case." I frowned, which instantly sent a shot of pain surging through the side of my head.

"All due respect, Mr. Carmichael," she playfully mocked me, "If you don't take it easy now, you'll be even less capable of getting work done later. Trust me. Taking some time to rest will do your brain good. See how quickly that headache snuck up on you?" She shot me a knowing glance as I gripped the side of my head, like that would somehow ease the pain coursing through my dome.

"We'll make sure he gets as much rest as possible, Doctor. Thank you so much for everything," Mique chimed in like she was runnin' shit. I had to give it to her, though. She'd been right by my side since I woke up, shortly after arriving here what felt like days ago, but was more realistically several hours.

Satisfied that I had an ample team to enforce her instructions, the doctor made her exit and said a nurse would be in soon with my discharge paperwork.

"Nigga, you keep watchin' her ass and Niq is gon' make sure you wind up right back in this bitch. You know she has Bee's ass to handle her lightweight and shit."

That nigga Savage was always on some other shit, but I didn't have the energy to go back and forth with his ass.

"Bruh, ain't shit wrong with looking. I'm just makin' sure I didn't lose my vision or anything. Anyway, ain't shit another chick can do for me except remind me how much I wanna dig Niq out the minute her ass is all healed up."

"TMI—I soooo didn't need to hear that," Mique huffed, rolling her eyes before disappearing out of the private triage area where they had my ass laid up.

"Bruh, shit been crazy for a while, but at least you got some good shit to lay on Niq," Savage changed the subject.

"No doubt. I know she's still gonna feel some type of way because I kept certain things from her, but shit, it's all a dead issue now—literally."

"True shit. But ay, I gotta burn out so I can hit the spot and be back before lil' man gets outta school. Crazy shit, bruh. Gotta schedule damn near everything I gotta do around bein' there for him...."

Savage's gaze shifted to the window and for a quick second, he got lost in his thoughts. I knew that look. It was the *"thoughts of Emani"* look.

"Hell yeah. It's hard work, but it looks good on you, bruh. Lil' man is lucky to have a real nigga in his life now," I encouraged my boy.

I couldn't even lay claim to having the fucked up kinda life that street legends were born from, but Savage? That nigga literally came from the bottom, had to fight his way through so many lows before he finally reached the high he was on now. Only thing missing was a baddie at his side, but technically, he had that shit too. He and Beautiful's Mayweather ass just needed to get their shit together. Truth was, they were both control freaks that refused to lose control and just let love do its thing. I'm not sayin' shit with me and Niq was picture perfect, but we had the hardest part out the way: I knew she was the one for me, and the same was true for her.

"Aight tho, I'm out, and hit my line later 'bout ya pops."

We dapped up and Savage took off to head for our spot in Richmond. He wasn't even gone a good five minutes before I had another visitor taking his place—well, two visitors.

"Yinc!"

"Short stack, what it do?"

It caused major pain to smile, but I didn't give a fuck. Essence was literally the light of my life right about now, and just seeing her made me forget about all the bullshit we'd been fighting our way through lately.

"Wumpy come see you, Yinc!" she beamed, pushing her little teddy bear, Rumpy, in my direction as Niq's mom led her closer to my bed.

Promise had really kept her word about staying clean and, more importantly, staying around for Niq and Essence. Truth be told, I don't know how the hell I would've been able to properly look after Essence with Niq still in the hospital if Promise hadn't been there to help me carry the load.

"So, what's the verdict, Linc?" Promise inquired about my condition.

"All clear. Just waitin' on my paperwork so I can get up out this bed and get back to business."

Yeah, I know the doctor said rest and all, but fuck all that. I was gonna work while I rested— how 'bout that?

"Well, we just left Aniqa at home not too long ago. I fixed breakfast and straightened the place up some while this little doll colored and read her mama a story."

"We go see Chuck E, Yinc?" Essence chimed, her little face lighting up like she'd just remembered something.

"Sweetie, Linc doesn't feel good, but maybe when he gets better, okay?"

Essence turned her little smile into a frown, dropped her head, and did that little pout that always made a nigga's chest tight. I know she wasn't mine by DNA, but this lil' girl had me wrapped around her finger, and I think she'd probably figured it out too.

"How 'bout this. I'll see if we can get up with Chuck E. in a few days after I get some rest, deal?" I smiled down at her and held my hand out for our lil' pinky swear.

"Deal!"

She wrapped her little finger around mine, sealing the deal. Now, I just had to hope I'd be good to take her because she would not only remember, but remind me to make sure I didn't forget.

"How is she doing, anyway?" I turned my attention to Promise to check on Niq's condition.

"About the same, but she got some good news today. Looks like she'll finally be able to come out the brace and wires in a few weeks."

I knew it was killing Niq to be laid up in the bed unable to talk, and I could only imagine how much she was gonna talk my head off the minute those wires came off her jaws. Hopefully, my good news would give her a reason to smile through the pain, though.

"So umm...did you guys get everything taken care of?" Promise inquired. Thankfully, I had nothing but positives to give her.

I remember when I first found Promise after she'd been missing from Niq's life for too long. Fucked up doesn't begin to describe the condition she was in, but Pops taught me a long time ago to search a person's eyes for the truth. I did just that with her, and when all I saw was a remorseful love for Niq, I knew I'd do anything in my power to make sure Niq never had to wonder if her mom was okay again. I told Promise I'd always keep it a buck with her because I wanted her to do the same with me, so she knew exactly what my mission was the night before. Soft-spoken as she was, Promise wanted the people that kept fuckin' with Niq dead just as much as the rest of us.

"Done deal. For sure, this time."

Finding out that Tiara was Kappo's daughter opened my eyes to the fact that I'd done something I always said I'd never do: let the pussy distract me from the real shit that was going on. I felt fucked up knowing that I let some good dome throw me off my square to the point where so much foul shit slipped right past me. Felt even worse that Niq had become a target, used as a pawn in the bullshit we'd been dealing with. I had some dope shit planned to help make up for it all, though. Honestly, Niq coulda been popped smoke on a nigga, but the fact that she stuck it out let me know she was a real one—even if I had to hear her mouth about it.

Peaceful and copacetic was the kinda life I wanted for me and mine, and it felt like we were finally getting there. Mique was home, Kappo and Tiara were no more, we'd recovered most of the money Kappo hit up the spots in Richmond and Charlotte for, my baby was recovering well, and most importantly, I could tell her we'd snatched up her justice and put her mind at ease.

Tiara was a schemin' ass bitch that was smarter than I gave her credit for, but for snatching up my princess and running my girl off the road, she got just what the fuck she deserved. I felt just a lil' fucked up that Kappo's wife had to bring a new baby into the world as a widow, but shit, she'd have to take the hand she was dealt up with God. She had the misfortune of marrying a fraud ass nigga, but hey, we all live and learn, right?

Savage and I always joked that this life chose us way before we could ever choose it, and that was true to an extent. Pops lived and breathed the life of a boss long before I even knew what the fuck that was, and while I was my own man and had a long list of shit I planned to do to make my own mark in the world, I didn't regret a single step on my path thus far.

"We color, Yinc!"

Tearing me from my thoughts, Essence did her best to climb up onto the bed next to me, box of crayons tucked under her arm. Promise helped her up and got her settled next to me, then stepped back and let us have our moment, flashing what I knew was a smile of gratitude as she watched Essence go to work showing me how to stay in the lines.

Everything happens for a reason, and Moms always told me people came into your life for reasons and seasons. We'd all been through a lot, both in business and in our personal lives, and I was glad to have a team of people that mattered the most still standing and riding with me for many seasons to come. Shit, I even looked at Mique in a new light after all this and felt that no matter what, baby sis had my back and wanted the same thing everyone else wanted: happiness.

Essence was just flipping the page to a picture of Doc McStuffins patching up an injured puppy when my phone buzzed in the plastic bag provided by the ER staff when I first came in. I nodded and pointed Promise in the right direction so she could retrieve it and pass it to me. *Just the call I've been waiting for.*

"What's good, Pops?"

Epilogue

Aniqa

Two Months Later...

"One piping hot bowl of Chicken noodle soup, minus the chicken, just the way you like it, sweetie."

I can't even count the number of times I wished for moments like this, moments when my mother would drop everything she was doing and nurse me back to health. Promise had been a much-appreciated addition to my life as of late. Don't get me wrong, what we have is nowhere near the perfect mother-daughter relationship, but if I've learned anything about life, I've learned there is no such thing as "perfect."

"Uh ohhh, you make a mess, Mommy!"

I remember a time when my baby girl didn't have a single word to utter. Had me and a few others worried that she was suffering some sort of developmental delay that precluded her from talking at all, but once again, God touched my situation at just the right time and had my baby girl bless us with the most beautiful voice ever. Now, the only time Essie was quiet was when she was asleep. I could never tire of hearing her sweet little voice, though.

"Looks like mommy needs a big baby bib, huh short stack?"

Linc. A man who stepped up when most other dudes would have kept it moving right on past me. A man who refuses to let me half-ass anything. A man who talks cash money shit and has the motive means to back it up.

People say there's always a calm before a storm, but when your life feels like a nonstop barrage of Cat-5 hurricanes, you start to wonder if you'll ever get even a tiny sliver of that calm. That used to be me. Used to be my entire existence. No peace, calm, rainbows, or sunny days. Too many times to count, I found myself on the cusp of wishing THAT day was my last. I felt like there was no way whatever came after life could be any worse than the life I was cursed with, and I just wanted to lay down, go to sleep, and never wake up again—almost.

See, lots of people think when a female becomes a mother at a young age, it's her "punishment" for being grown and fast. Her eternal chastisement for trying to live the life of a grown woman with the mentality of a little girl. Day in and day out, that's all I heard when I became pregnant with

Essence, but little did I know, what felt like a curse would turn out to be a beacon of light, a hope that would give me a reason NOT to give up, not to give in to the temptation to close my eyes one last time for an eternal rest.

Essence may have come into my life while I still had the mindset of a confused young girl, but unbeknownst to me, she was a blessing that pulled me into womanhood, giving me no other choice but to grow up and welcome the maturity that came with being a grown woman. She taught me to love unconditionally, to open my heart and receive that same kind of unconditional love from another person. I spent so many years hoping I'd get that kind of love from Je'Marcus, but when it came down to it, he served his purpose, spent his season in my life, and showed we what love *was not* so I'd recognize and appreciate it when it came along. God is always right on time, giving you exactly what you need at the precise moment you need it, and I'll be forever grateful He saw fit to bring Linc and I together that day in Walgreens.

A year ago, I was stuck in a dead-end relationship that had me in fear of my life almost daily, living in what felt like the worst psychological prison with no aspirations other than to make it through each day without feeling the wrath of the abusive father of my daughter. Now? I'm just a few weeks away from finishing up my first year of college with a 3.8 GPA (damn Quantitative Statistics class kicked my ass!), have a loving and healthy home for myself and Essence, a guy who loves me for me and showers Essie with a genuine fatherly love like it's his blood coursing through her veins, and I have the mother I missed so much time with. Add my bestie, Beautiful, my handsome nephew, TJ, and my second mother, Ms. Khadra to the mix and I feel like I'm blessed and highly favored a hundred times over. Even Savage's crazy behind is a welcome addition as he does something no dude before him has been able to do: tames the Tasmanian temper that is Beautiful Mudarris.

Every single thing that tried to pull me under water was put to rest—all because of Linc. So yup, life's good, and even if me and Linc's mother never see eye to eye, I'll still appreciate each and every day I'm blessed to wake up with my perfectly imperfect family.

"I have something for you, sweetie...when you're done eating, of course," my mom interrupted my jagged trip down memory lane.

Linc found something to keep Essie occupied back in her room, so after Promise made a quick exit, it was just me, the TV, and the intricately ornate keepsake box she set on the table before she left the room. Easing forward, I pulled the box onto my lap, released the thick clasp, and opened it to see what sort of surprise awaited me...and boy was it a surprise!

Finally, after I don't know how many years of wondering, after countless pleas that seemed to fall on deaf ears, I had the answer to a question that weighed heavily on my head and heart for as long as I could remember. They say there are just a few degrees of separation between all living things. Reading the words on the paper in my hand over and over again, that theory never felt more true as I saw that I shared a father with someone I knew all too well: JaMiya Watford— sister to my baby daddy, Je'Marcus!

Beautiful

"Would you like more to drink, Sampson?"

Leave it to my mother to be the perfect, Suzy-homemaker host anytime she had company. Savage's ass better not get too used to it though because as far as I was concerned, he could get his ass up and refill his own damn drink. Ain't no bottle service, bihh!

"See that? Bee, you need to watch and pay attention. You might learn something, like how you're supposed to treat ya man!"

See? His ass always had some slick shit to say!

"Well, when I see MY man, I'll treat him as such!"

You know I stay with that comeback, right?

"Yeah, aight. We gon' see if you still got all that mouth tonight," he mumbled just loud enough for me to hear, but low enough that neither my mom nor the kids heard it.

Okay, so yes, I finally gave in and called Savage back, but not to beg for his attention or no crazy shit like that. Since I had nothing but time to think —along with daily comments from the peanut gallery that was comprised of my mom, Niq, and even Linc on occasion— I realized maybe I *was* being a brat about this thing between me and Savage. I also realized the main reason I kept pushing his ass away too. Because I kept expecting him to be the same kinda fuck-up that Tyleek was. I don't even wanna speak on the way that nigga crushed my heart—no, more like ripped it out of my chest. Let's just say, he made it so any and every nigga I cross paths with for the rest of my life will get a side eye so serious they're gonna think I'm cock-eyed.

Aside from TJ's constant badgering about when he was gonna see him again, the other thing that finally made me pick up the phone was Dre, whom I learned was officially Savage's adopted son at this point.

"Hol' up, lemme help y'all with that!" Savage called across the yard to TJ and Dre, who were trying to raise the kiddie basketball goal up a few inches. Dre had TJ by about three inches in height, so he could easily dunk on the hoop where we currently had it set for TJ. "Lemme get some more of that potato salad too, because I know your ass is headed to the kitchen again," he teased, slapping my thigh as he stood up and jogged across the yard.

He was right, though. Damn right I was about to claim another helping of my mama's macaroni and cheese. By the time I made it back to the table out on my mom's patio, Savage had both boys trying to guard him while he easily made jump shots over their heads. Super cute, but he could have at least missed a few shots to make the boys feel like they were doing something.

"You might not want to admit it, but he's just what you need, daughter of mine. And TJ too."

Okay actually, it was my mom that was the final straw in my decision to finally call Savage back. Truth be told, she planned this little cookout specifically for him. Said she was tired of seeing me mope around even more mad at the world than usual. She pulled my card, too; told me Savage wasn't to blame for the shit Tyleek took me through, and that I couldn't run from happiness forever.

"He's aight, Ma."

Glad I listened and let her plan this little thing, too because I can't even lie— Savage looked fine as fuck today, and it made me realize just how much I missed him. Was I gonna give in and try to do this couple thing with him? Yes. Was I looking forward to letting him do any and everything he wanted to my body later tonight? Damn right! I wasn't about to tell his ass all that, though. Let his ass sweat a little.

"Just alright, huh? Sweetheart, hear this, and hear me well. Love looks so good on you, baby. Has your skin glowing and everything, so do me a favor. Stop being so darn mean and let that man love you the way he wants to. You know you want him to." Mama winked, then brushed a kiss on my cheek before heading inside.

We still had a good ways to go before we had that whole blended family thing going on that Niq and Linc had finally seemed to master, but Mama was right. Savage was good for me and TJ, and seeing the way he was with little Dre, I had no doubts that he knew when to set that thuggish street shit to the side and be about his business at home. I was actually impressed with how he seemed to fall right into this fatherhood thing and was doing his best to give Dre a good life. So, who knows what the future holds for me? For us? All I know is I can't cheat my present because of my past, and I won't ever know if Savage is the one for me unless I give him a chance to show me what he's capable of, right?

So, here goes. Officially throwing caution to the wind to see if there really is a such thing as a happily ever after in this crazy thing called hood love. Y'all pray we don't kill each other in the process!

Savage

"Dre! C'mere!"

Aight, so for the most part, a nigga could do this fatherhood thing in his sleep. This lil' nigga Dre really coulda been my seed. Smart as shit and a go-getter that was up and dressed in the mornings before my feet even hit the floor. I ain't gon' lie. It felt good as shit bein' out on the court, shootin' around with the lil' homie and showin' him how to ace that layup that niggas just couldn't touch. Like I said—for the most part.

It was this discipline and enforcement that a nigga wasn't feelin. I had no issues sendin' a nigga to get his last rites in the streets. Matter fact, I enjoyed it. I didn't like havin' to play the bad guy at home, though.

"Nah, what I tell you about that head?"

Dre had a lil' timidness about him that I guess was aight for a lil' boy, but I was raising a man so as far as I was concerned, it was never too early for lil' man to start acting the part.

"H-hold my head high. Always I-look a m-man in the eye," he stammered.

Oh yeah, that stuttering thing? Turns out he'd been doing it ever since he started talking. Not on my watch, though. Bee's mom, Ms. Khadra, put me in touch with a speech therapist that was supposed to be the best of the best, so I had my lil' man set up for weekly sessions to get him right.

"Right. Even when you mess up or make a mistake, you look a man in the eye and own it. You don't hide from or back down from nothing. Feel me?"

He nodded his agreement and shifted his eyes from his socks up to my face.

"Aight, now why does your teacher think you don't wanna participate in this class project?"

I pushed the half-completed project his teacher sent home in an envelope into his hand. He gave it a quick glance and almost as though someone had hit a switch, tears pooled along the edge of his eyelids.

"Nah, man. No tears. Wipe your face and tell me what's goin' on. Why you don't wanna do your work?"

Dre fought off a few sniffles, reached over to get a tissue off my sofa table to clean his face, then came back to stand in front of me.

"Well?" I pressed him. I was starting to notice that he tended to shut down and get quiet when he didn't wanna deal with stuff, but I needed my lil' man to be more vocal and speak his mind.

"I c-can't do it."

"You what? I don't know what *can't* means. Tell me what can't means."

"I c-can't."

"My man, we can do anything we put our minds to, so can't don't exist. Either we choose to do things, or we choose not to. And if we don't have what we need to do things, we go get it. So, are you choosing not to do the project?" I quizzed him.

"But e-everybody else—"

"We don't worry 'bout everybody else, right?"

"I can't do it, Sam!"

My lil' man was back in tears, so I figured I'd ease up some. This had to be more than him just refusing to do some lil' project on construction paper, so I needed to find out.

"C'mere, man."

I patted my lap so we could do the father-son, heart-to-heart thing. Never heard of no shit like that a day in my life, but Bee was schoolin' me on how to do that nurturing thing kids needed. She said it helped them grow into empathetic and well-adjusted members of society—whatever the hell that meant.

"Talk to me, lil' man. Why do you feel like you can't do it?"

"I don't have a m-mommy no more, Sam..."

Shit. I didn't know what to say to that, but when I pulled the additional slip of paper from the envelope, I understood what Dre meant. The class was doing a project in preparation for Mother's Day, and each student was supposed to make a picture of their mom to hang on the class bulletin board.

"I c-can't make no picture if I c-can't see my mommy..." Dre mumbled, and I felt like shit for overlooking something so obvious.

Sliding Dre off my lap and sitting him on the loveseat, I went back into my hall closet and dug around in a box I had recently placed on the top shelf. Took me a few minutes to find what I was looking for because it was stuck between some papers, but once I did, I put everything back in its place and joined Dre on the loveseat.

"My fault, lil' man, but I tell you what. I'mma make sure you can see your moms whenever you need to. You can take her everywhere you go if you want. Here."

I passed Dre the most recent picture I had of Emani. It was actually a picture of the two of them at some park. Found it when I was helping her old neighbor, Ms. Pamela, clean her place out after she passed. Guess there was a reason I came across it, though I didn't know it at the time.

Dre sat frozen for a good three minutes, just swept up in the fresh image of him and his mom. I wondered what was going through his lil' head, wondered if he remembered the exact moment they took the pic. I didn't ask him, though, because that was his business. With him losing his moms at such a young age, I wasn't sure which memories would stick and which would fade away. I wanted him to be able to hold on to as many as he could, though.

"You good, lil' man?" I pressed him when a whole five minutes had passed, and he nodded his head with a weak smile.

"Can I t-talk to my mommy, Sam?"

The hell? Talk to her how?

"You wanna talk to your moms?"

"Yeah. Through the 'puter. See, look."

Dre padded across the floor and over to the lil' nook where my computer was set up, climbed up in the chair, and then pointed to the round lens of the monitor's built-in camera.

"Here. My friend Thomas s-said his mommy can s-see him in here, and he t-talks to her. Can I t-talk to Mommy?"

Bee told me there's gon' be a lotta times when you gotta fake it with kids, just to see the smiles on their faces, even when the shit don't make no sense, so I guessed this was one of those times. I was cool with it, though. If it would put a smile on lil' man's face, he could make as many videos as he wanted, whenever he wanted.

The minute Dre knew he was on camera and "talking to his mommy," it was like he came out of his lil' shell. I told him we could record the videos and send 'em up to heaven for his mom to watch, and that was all he needed to hear. I stepped back into my room and laid across the bed to give him some privacy, but I heard him tellin' Emani all about school, how Ms. Sheree makes the best waffles he's ever had (he even apologized for it being better than Emani's), how Bee's son, TJ, is smart for a lil' kid and he can't wait to play Uno with him again, and how much he likes his new room because he can see up to heaven through his lil' skylight. He was on cam so long a nigga dozed off, waking up to him shaking me to turn the camera off and make him a snack. Best feeling in the world.

If you would've told me that I'd be somebody's daddy even two years ago, I woulda laughed your ass clear outta town. If you would've said I'd be adopting someone else's seed, shit, ain't no way in hell. But here I was, raising a lil' boy that I low-key felt should've been my seed in the first place.

I always said I didn't wanna be one of those niggas that had kids scattered between multiple houses and multiple women. Said the only place I'd plant my seed was in a woman that had the ring and my last name, but it looked like God had other plans for me when it came to fatherhood. I wasn't mad, though, because in just the few months I'd been lookin' after Dre, a nigga felt...complete.

This past year's been crazy for me and my peoples, in so many ways, but the main lesson I learned is that you can't live life in reverse, so I'm facing forward, focused on the road before me, and lookin' forward to what's waiting at the next intersection for me, Dre, TJ, and Beautiful's crazy ass. I'm that nigga Savage— I always get what I want, feel me?

Linc

"So, it's all over, Daddy?"

Much like the rest of us, Mique was shocked to hear that Pops' legal worries were null and void. Turns out the meeting with the DA was to inform Pops and his attorney that the case against him had been dropped. Something about previous witness statements being deemed inadmissible. Pops' attorney did some digging and learned that the DA received a mountain of intel from an undercover federal agent that not only cleared Pops' name, but also pointed to Kappo as the person they should have been investigating. In the eyes of the law, every legit business entity that bore the Carmichael name was just that—legit.

My gut was on point about the nigga Jason, too. He was a fed, but somewhere along the way, I guess he decided he was gonna switch sides. Turns out Jason was the son of Gino, Pops' former right-hand that Kappo set up to look like he betrayed Pops. Talk about six degrees of separation. That and the fact that he developed a crush on LaMique steered his actions in the end. I wasn't too fond of him crushin' on my sister, but with Pops being cleared and us being free to resume business as usual, Jason was a good dude in my book.

A good portion of this "intel" Jason got came from none other than Paxton, his Pops (Patrick), and Megga (Kappo's cousin). For that reason, those niggas were safe for now, too. Savage was pissed because he was looking forward to adding to his body count, but shit, I was relieved at how it all worked out. It meant we'd done a sufficient job of shaking our weak links and cleaning house to make sure everyone on our team was really *for us.*

All charges were dismissed with prejudice, meaning shit was a dead issue.

"All done and put to rest, baby girl."

Pops pulled Mique and my mother into his chest. We were all relieved that Pops was in the clear, but I think they took the threat to his freedom harder than me because he was their everything. Shit, I knew the risks that came with the life we lived and the way we made our money, so my mindset was always to protect my Pops at all costs, but be ready to assume the throne if need be. Either way, seeing my sis and moms relieved let me know me and Pops were both on our shit as the men of the family.

"Thank the Lord for delivering us from old trials and tribulations, and blessing us with new beginnings," Moms beamed, reaching over to rub the protruding womb where our newest family addition was baking.

I don't think I seen Moms happier than the minute she learned her first grandchild was on the way. Hold up, because I know what y'all are thinking. It ain't me. Essence might not be mine biologically, but shit, that lil' girl gives me a run for my money every day. Plus, I don't think I'm ready to share my attention for her with another kid anyway. Me and Niq are good on that "fruitful and multiply" thing for now.

LaMique is the one that's gonna give birth to the next link in the Carmichael family chain. Turns out that nigga Kappo got the last laugh on at least one thing. Remember how I said I was gonna get to the bottom of why her ass was up in the hospital while the law was all over her shit out in Colorado? Turns out that's why. She had some kinda female thing goin' on, and when she went in to see what was up, they told her she was gonna be a mother.

Honestly, I didn't know how to feel about it. Of course, I was looking forward to meeting my new lil' niece or nephew, but to know the lil' kid would carry Kappo's blood had me feeling some type of way. Part of me felt like that shit would blow up down the line and bring more bullshit to our doorstep, but trust that between me, Pops, and Savage, we were ready for whatever and whomever felt bold enough to fuck with our shit.

"Yinc! We go see doggie, Yinc!"

Yes, folks. I finally convinced Niq to give this family dinner thing at my parent's spot another shot. Well, more like bribed. It was supposed to be a Mother's Day dinner, but Moms wasn't about to let anyone else up in her kitchen, so she wound up making dinner to celebrate herself. Typical.

So, in honor of Mother's Day, Niq agreed to sit down and try to break bread with Moms again, but only after she finessed me for a high-dollar value item that we're gonna just let remain undisclosed. I appreciated her effort, though, and it was just further proof that she was just the right chick for me.

I had to work twice as hard to get Moms to agree to behave herself, though. From her point of view, shit didn't start going left in our lives until Niq came onto the scene, which was partially true, but none of the shit that happened was Niq's fault per se. Moms and I had a full-throttle, no-holds barred heart to heart about Niq and Essence because, quite frankly, they weren't going anywhere. Moms even walked away and left me looking like a fool in the middle of the restaurant; pretty sure she cursed a nigga out on her way out too. I gave her that, though, because I understood she just wanted the best for me, but I made her see that it was up to me to decide who and what was best for myself. She finally got it, though, and agreed to be nice to Niq as long as she was nice to her. That was a start, right?

"Doggie where, short stack?"

Moms was allergic, so we never had any type of pet growing up, but once she dragged me to the front door, I saw that one of my neighbors had a kiddie pool full of the cutest lil' Yorkie puppies. I wasn't exactly sold on the idea of a lil' furball pissin' in my spot, but judging by the way both Niq and short stack's faces were all lit up, I knew I'd probably be outvoted on this particular issue.

"How 'bout this: we'll go see the puppies after we finish eating, deal?"

Two pinky swears later, we were all seated around the formal dining table Moms swore she didn't get to use often enough because the whole family was rarely under the same roof. I invited Bee and Savage, but lil' Dre had a game and they were going to visit Bee's mom after, so we let them do the blended family thing. If I had to guess, Bee's wild ass was probably on her second strike and dangerously close to being kicked out the park. I don't care what those two said: they were crazy in love with each other and would set some shit on fire if either tried to step out with someone else.

With Niq to my left and Essence to my right, I felt like I was the glue that was gonna keep our lil' family together by any means necessary. Best feeling in the world.

"Let's bow our heads so we can bless the food," Moms instructed, but before we could get the prayer started, the doorbell rang. Mique was closest to the door, so she went to see who'd interrupted what I hoped would be a peaceful family dinner. When she returned with who I considered an unwelcome guest, I just knew that notion of peace was about to be challenged.

"Oh hey, Angela! Good to see you? Is everything okay? We were just about to have dinner. Would you two like to join us?"

You heard Moms right, two of them. As in this messy ass chick showed up unannounced at what she knew was dinner time. Moms was a creature of habit, so no matter whether she'd set the table for two or ten, dinner was served at the same time daily. I got that she was Moms' best friend and all, but she knew that shit was rude as hell. That's what phones were for.

You know what her ass did, right? Eagerly accepted Mom's invitation to join us for dinner—her and her *"plus one."* Of course, leave it to my petty ass sister to start some shit. You'd think she would wanna take a break and leave the petty cape hanging in the closet being that she was just kidnapped by her crazy ass baby daddy and his side-piece daughter, right? Wrong.

Just as Pops retrieved an extra chair to accommodate Angela's slick ass and her tagalong, Mique leaned down and whispered into my ear on her way back to her own seat.

"Linc....umm...why Ms. Angela's lil' boy look just like you, though?"

~ THE END ~

READERS: THE REAL MVPS

Thanks again for your rocking with me! I'd love to hear what you thought of this story, so be sure to stop by **Amazon** or **Goodreads** and leave a review.

Drop me an email at info@tyshajordyn.com and let me know what's on your mind.

Tysha Jordyn

 Follow Me!

Let's stay connected!

Facebook: www.facebook.com/tysha.jordyn

GoodReads: www.goodreads.com/tyshajordyn

Instagram/Twitter: @tysha_jordyn

Website: www.tyshajordyn.com

 JOIN MY TEAM TODAY!

Get 5 More Books COMPLETELY FREE

and Exclusive Reader Material

Building a relationship with my readers is hands down, one of the most rewarding aspects of being a writer. I LOVE hearing from you and sharing tidbits of my writing journey with you all! I occasionally send out short messages with details on upcoming releases, advance reading opportunities, special offers, VIP Reader-exclusive giveaways, and other bits of news relating to past series and new projects.

If you join my VIP Reader list, I'll send you the following items **completely FREE:**

1. A copy of *Something In My Heart*
2. A copy of *You Should Be Here*, a **VIP-Reader exclusive** novelette ($2.99 retail price). Exclusive to my VIP Reader list - you can't get this anywhere else.
3. A copy of *Chasing Kingston: A Lawless Love*
4. A copy of *The Streets of Love*
5. A copy of *Boss: The Miami Connect*

You get all this content **for free** by joining my VIP reader list. Scan the code below to add yourself!

TYSHA JORDYN

Book Order Form

Would you like to add my books to your library, organization, or personal collection? Place your order using the information/form below:

Title	Cost	Quantity	Total Due Per Title
Love The Way You Thug Me	$10		
Love The Way You Thug Me 2	$10		
Love, Betrayal, & Dirty Money	$10		
Chase & Kassidy: All Eyes On Us	$10		
His Majesty 1	$10		
His Majesty 2	$10		
His Majesty 3	$10		
Crushin' On A Boss: The Streets or Love	$10		
Crushin' On A Boss 2: The Streets or Love	$12		
Crushin' On A Boss 3: The Streets or Love	$15		
Crushin' On A Boss 4 - Finale: The Streets or Love	$15		
Bulletproof Gods: Money Over Everything	$15		
Bulletproof Gods 2 - Finale: Money Over Everything	$12		
His Heart Belongs to Me	$10		
GRAND TOTAL FOR ALL TITLES ORDERED			

| Name: |
| Phone: |
| Email: |

FREE SHIPPING ON ALL BOOKS to any US or APO/FPO address

Where to Send Orders:

Order requests can be sent via email to **info@tyshajordyn.com**

Ordering 10 or more books?

Contact us for bulk discount information at info@tyshajordyn.com

To get exclusive and advance looks at some of our top releases:

Visit the link: (App Store): **http://bit.ly/2iYOdnZ**

Visit the link (Google Play): **http://bit.ly/2h4Jw9X**

CPSIA information can be obtained
at www.ICGtesting.com
Printed in the USA
LVOW10s2139171017
552760LV00017B/568/P